ONLY HALF
HUMAN

The Cambion Tales
Book 1

ONLY HALF
HUMAN

By
NATHANIEL WRIGHT

BATTLE CROW BOOKS

Copyright © 2022 Nathaniel Wright
First Edition: October 2022

Editing by P. J. Hoover
Copy editing by Karen Robinson
Cover art by Casey Gerber

Print ISBN 979-8-9867098-2-6
Ebook ISBN 979-8-9867098-0-2
Kindle ISBN 979-8-9867098-1-9

Visit natewrightsbooks.com for more information.

Acknowledgment

Thanks to my beta readers Paula, Penny, Jake, Paul, all the members of the Toledo Writers club but especially John and Cameron, and my sister Elizabeth for providing feedback and encouraging me to keep writing.

Table of Contents

1

The Witch

This is going to sound crazy, but I'm only half human.

Shocking, right? It was for me when I first found out. Before that horrible night, I was just an average high school girl. My biggest worries were the kind most teenagers have, like surviving the first week of sophomore year or making new friends.

I stood by my locker, glancing down the hall toward a trio of girls. How was it that no matter what outfits they threw together, they always looked cool? I frowned down at my own clothing. Pink tee shirt—a little faded and definitely nothing fancy. Jeans with holes in the knees, not by choice—all my jeans were like that. The start of a new school year was a good enough reason to make some new friends. But seeing how much better those girls were dressed, I wasn't so sure. Still, I put on a friendly smile and approached.

"Hey," I said. "I heard you guys were going to the movies tonight. Mind if I come too?"

Their conversation stopped as the three girls turned to me. I tried not to flinch as they scrutinized my thrift store outfit.

Finally, their leader spoke. "Sorry, Lesley. We've already reserved our seats. It would be kind of a hassle to squeeze you in last minute. You know how it is."

My smile faded. "Oh. Maybe some other time, then." I turned and trudged away.

Behind me, one of the other girls snickered. "Maybe if her deadbeat dad was still around, poor Lesley could afford some real clothes."

I meandered through the crowd of students, back to where my friend Phyllis was waiting. Her forehead was dotted with acne despite the pimple cream she used, and her hair seemed even more frizzy than usual.

"Rejected?" she asked.

"Rejected," I muttered.

Phyllis tilted her head. "I still don't get why you suddenly want to be friends with them. You've got, like, nothing in common."

I sighed. "I'm sick of being just some loser. Maybe that would change if I were friends with someone cool."

She offered a smile. "At least you have another loser for company."

"You say that like it's a good thing."

Phyllis gasped, pretending to be offended, before we both burst into laughter. "I know what will cheer you up. We should stop at Mrs. McKee's after school. She'll probably have cookies."

"Hmm, I don't know. My mom doesn't want me visiting her anymore." But the draw of Mrs. McKee's fresh-baked cookies was hard to resist.

* * *

The bell rang, and students poured out through the school's front entrance. Side by side, Phyllis and I strode along the sidewalk through the neighborhood.

Phyllis sighed. "I can't believe we had to do an algebra quiz today. It's still just the first week of school!"

"Right?" I said. "I'm having a quiz in history class tomorrow, and—" I stopped and pointed along the sidewalk. "Is that Mrs. McKee's pet ferret?"

A small furry head was peeking around the corner of a house. When he saw me, the white-furred animal came running and huddled against my shins. "Aw, did you get lost?" I scooped him up in my arms. "I guess we're going to Mrs. McKee's house after all."

We headed down the street, and Phyllis knocked on the door of a small cottage. A wrinkled face peered out at us. "Phyllis, Lesley, hello," Mrs. McKee said. "Oh, you found Snowball! Thank goodness. Come in, please, come in."

Doilies and knick-knacks decorated the living room, and the wonderful smell of cookies baking wafted in from the kitchen. I set Snowball down, and the ferret ran to Mrs. McKee, pawing at her knees. "There you are, you little rascal," the white-haired woman said. "I wondered where you'd gotten to." She winked at him.

I scrunched my brow. Something about the way Mrs. McKee had winked gave me the strangest idea—that she'd actually sent Snowball out *on purpose*. I shook my head, dismissing the silly notion.

Snowball relaxed, stretching himself out on the floor. Mrs. McKee turned to us. "I was hoping you two would come by today. You especially, Lesley." She headed into the kitchen.

3

I followed. "Why me especially?" I asked.

She pulled a tray of cookies from the oven and set them on the counter. "Because," she said, "I sense a great change is upon you."

Typical Mrs. McKee. She was a bit eccentric and claimed to be a witch. Phyllis and I usually went along with it, letting her read our palms or cast sheep's teeth like dice to tell our fortunes. "Oh, uh, that's cool," I said politely.

"Aren't you curious to know more about this change?" the old woman asked.

Not really, I thought. "Um, sure."

She beckoned me to take a seat at the kitchen table and spread a deck of cards in front of me. They weren't playing cards but tarot cards, each illustrated with a different scene. The imagery was straight out of fairy tales, depicting knights and kings, swords and chalices, dragons and monsters. Mrs. McKee sat across from me and gathered the cards into a neat stack. "These cards can reveal truths about you and perhaps tell us about this coming change." She looked me in the eye. "Do you want to know your truth, Lesley?"

I hadn't noticed him climb up, but Snowball was perched on the woman's shoulder. The ferret watched me with a look just as intense as Mrs. McKee's. A weird chill crept through me. "My truth? Uh, yeah, I guess."

She drew a card from the top of the deck and laid it in front of me. Mrs. McKee grinned as she looked at the card. "Ha! I thought so. Your mother is a witch like me. That's why she didn't want you coming here—because she doesn't want you to find out." She winked. "But you didn't hear it from me."

My mom *wasn't* a witch—at least, I didn't think she was. Of course, I wouldn't know if she *secretly* did witchy things like reading palms or consulting tarot cards, but I was pretty sure she didn't. I was too weirded out to say anything, though, so just I watched as Mrs. McKee drew another card and laid it next to the first.

"Ah, yes," she said, nodding gravely. "Your mother is about to return to Misty Hollow, and you will go with her. Perhaps this is the change I sense."

My jaw dropped. "Misty Hollow! How do you know about that?"

She laughed. "Believe me now, do you? And you thought I was just some batty old woman."

Slowly, I shook my head. "I-I must have mentioned my mom's stories to you before. That's how you know about Misty Hollow."

"Rationalize it however you like, dearie. But sooner or later you'll have to accept that the world is different from what you thought." Mrs. McKee paused. "Oh, and when you leave, could you not mention any of this to Phyllis? I cast a spell on her to keep our conversation private, and I'd like it to stay that way."

Glancing around, I realized Phyllis wasn't in the kitchen with me. "What? Where's Phyllis?"

"She's perfectly comfortable, I assure you. Eating a few cookies, I'd bet. Now, where were we?" Mrs. McKee drew a third card.

She paused, her eyes widening as she peered at the last tarot card. Snowball squeaked and scurried away. "What is this?" Mrs. McKee murmured. "Lesley, you used to have nightmares about demons?"

I almost fell out of my chair. "No... there's *no way* you could know about my nightmares. I've *never* told anyone except my mother."

"As I said, the cards reveal truths. But why is the deck showing me that you—" She looked at me. "Oh, of course. Now it all makes sense. That's why your father is never around." Mrs. McKee narrowed her eyes. "Lesley, I must ask you to leave."

"What? I don't understand—"

She pointed a bony finger at the door. "Leave, now!"

I scrambled from my seat and, before I knew it, was through the living room and out the front door. I nearly knocked Phyllis over. "Oh, thank god, there you are!"

She turned to me. "Lesley? Is something wrong?"

"What do you mean 'is something wrong?' In the kitchen, Mrs. McKee said—"

"What are you talking about? We were with Mrs. McKee in her living room, eating cookies the whole time."

* * *

I felt awkward trying to convince Phyllis that something strange had happened at Mrs. McKee's house, so I gave up. And I never got a chance to take that history test because the very next day, I came down with a terrible fever.

My room was dark except for the sunset glow seeping through the window blinds. My bedsheets lay rumpled around me, and sweat beaded on my forehead. A knock sounded on the door.

"Lesley?" my mother called.

"Mmf..." I groaned.

My mom came in, carrying a steaming mug. Rugby, a black-and-white border collie, trotted in after her. The dog hopped onto the bed, licking my face sympathetically. I reached up to scratch between his ears.

My mother held out the mug. "I brought you some more tea, sweetie."

I wrinkled my nose. She'd been giving me tea all day—she claimed it was some kind of herbal remedy. No amount of arguing had convinced her to give me real medicine. With a sigh, I propped myself up and took the mug in my hands. The hint of honey and cinnamon did nothing to hide the bitterness of whatever else she'd put in the concoction. Holding my nose, I drank it.

I set the mug aside. "Mom, can't you just take me to the doctor?"

For a long moment, she was silent. "I'm sure you'll feel better by tomorrow," my mother said. "How is that rash on your back doing?"

I rolled over, allowing my mom to pull aside the straps of my tank top. "It still itches, and I think it's spreading."

"Oh, it doesn't look so bad." The hesitation in her voice told me she was lying.

"Are you sure it's not getting worse?" I rolled back over and reached up to scratch an itch on my forehead. "Mom, seriously, why don't we just go to the doctor—"

She caught my wrist, pulling my hand away from my brow. For an instant, fear flashed in her eyes.

My mother let go of my wrist. "You're right, Lesley. If you're not feeling better by tomorrow, I'll take you to the doctor." She took the empty mug and headed to the door. Rugby followed at her side, whimpering up at her. "Goodnight, sweetie," my mom said, closing the door behind her.

I lay back down but didn't close my eyes. I couldn't stop thinking about the frightened look that had crossed my mother's face.

* * *

That night, I dreamed of demons. It was the same nightmare as from when I was little—the nightmare I'd never told anyone about except my mom. In the dream, demons surrounded me. Their hair was oily and matted, their skin red and slick with slime. Horns jutted from their brows, and their eyes burned with fire. The demons jeered and cackled as they grasped me with cold, clammy hands, their claws pricking my skin. I struggled against them, crying and screaming for my mother, but the demons wouldn't let go.

I gasped, opening my eyes. "Just a dream," I told myself. "It was just a dream." I'd thrown off my bedsheets, and my pajamas were soaked with sweat. My forehead itched like crazy, and the rash on my back felt like it was on fire. I sat up, reaching around to rub my back, and shuddered. The skin between my shoulders was covered in blisters. I pulled my hand away, hoping the warm, sticky feeling on my fingertips was just sweat and not blood. With my other hand, I reached up to scratch my itching forehead.

I felt something there and screamed. I leaped out of bed, dashing down the hall to the bathroom. I flicked on the light and screamed again when I saw my face in the mirror—saw the blood trickling from my blistered brow, saw what was emerging.

"I'm still dreaming," I told myself. "I have to still be dreaming!"

But it didn't feel like a dream this time.

My mom burst into the room. "Lesley?" Her eyes went wide. "No!"

The burning across my back turned to sharp, stabbing pain. I peered over my shoulder into the mirror. Between my tank top straps, the blisters on my back were bulging. A jab of pain sent me to my knees. "Mom, it hurts! It hurts!"

My mother dashed back into the hall and returned carrying a pouch. She set the bag down on the counter and dug through it. "It'll be okay, sweetie," she said. But her voice was shaking.

Inside the pouch was a collection of mismatched jars, bottles, and vials filled with powders and liquids. My mom filled a brass bowl with water and sprinkled in the contents of one vial, then another. I hugged myself, holding in another scream as pain clawed at my back. "Mom, what are you doing?"

"I'll explain later." She reached into the pouch and took out a polished wooden rod—what looked for all the world like a magic wand. She recited something as she waved the wand over the bowl, and I jumped as the water started boiling. Wisps of steam rose, filling my nostrils with a soothing smell. "Breathe it in," my mother said. "It will numb the pain."

I gasped in the strange vapors, and the pain across my back subsided. I looked in the mirror again. "No, this has to be a dream." I pinched myself on the arm. "Wake up!"

My mom took my hands in hers, tears glistening in her eyes. "You're not dreaming, sweetie."

I hissed as pain jabbed at my back. "Mom, please! What's going on?"

"Do you remember the stories I told you when you were younger, about Misty Hollow?"

I blinked. "But those were just fairy tales."

She shook her head. "No, Lesley. They were true. The fae *are* real, and... and Lesley, you are..." She bit her lip. "I should have prepared you more for this. But I thought I could prevent the transformation. I thought you'd never have to know."

"Mom, please! What's happening to me?"

She hesitated. "Lesley, your father, he... he was a demon."

My eyes widened, and I stumbled back as the pain returned. I screamed in horror at my reflection in the mirror as something sprouted through my blistered skin, reaching out from between my shoulder blades.

2

The Cambion

I stared blankly out the window of my mother's car as she drove through the countryside. The road bobbed over the hills, past fields and farmhouses and clumps of trees. I slumped in my seat, my arms crossed. The hood of my jacket was pulled down low to hide my forehead. Rugby was crouched in the back, next to a stack of boxes and some baskets of folded clothes.

My mom glanced at me. "Are you doing all right, Lesley?"

I frowned, keeping my gaze out the window.

She sighed. "Well, we're almost there."

My mother turned down a side road. The trees grew thicker as the road climbed uphill. As we crested the hill, my mom and Rugby seemed to relax. I gave her a look.

She slowed the car and pointed back the way we'd come. "See those runes carved in the trees at either side of the road?"

I glanced back at a few strange, angular shapes cut into the trunks.

"We're inside the protective wards," my mom explained. "We should be safe now."

My brow remained furrowed. Was this something I was supposed to know from the fairy tales she'd told me? If it was, I couldn't remember. I hadn't slept much after what had happened last night, and the day so far had been a blur. Until that moment, it hadn't even occurred to me to ask where we were going.

"Mom, where are you taking us? What is this place?"

"Surely you must have guessed by now."

My eyes widened. "Wait, do you mean..."

She nodded. "Yes, sweetie. We're going to Misty Hollow."

The road took us downhill, and the trees thinned. We passed by a cottage or two and emerged onto an avenue lined with little shops. I began to recall the stories my mother had once told. But I'd imagined Misty Hollow as a fantastic place of fairytale castles and haunted mansions, not as a normal-looking town. "This isn't what I expected."

"The havens have to look ordinary," my mother explained. "The fae don't want to raise suspicion in case humans wander in."

Humans—what I thought my mom and I were until last night. Part of me still couldn't believe what was happening. "I can't remember if you explained that in your stories. If humans show up, do the fae, like, put on disguises or something?"

"Some do, but others have to go hide. Alarms go off if anyone unwelcome crosses the wards." She sighed. "I'm just thankful the mayor is allowing *us* to come here. I don't know what I would have done otherwise."

I wondered if the magic wards kept anything else out. I pulled out my phone and sighed with relief when it still worked. Apparently I got coverage even inside magical boundaries.

My mom turned the car down a side street, and we drove past houses nestled among the trees. She pulled to a stop in front of a small brick house with a *Sold* sign in the front yard. My mom exited the car, and Rugby leaped out after her. The dog bounded this way and that across the front lawn, his nose to the ground as he sniffed excitedly.

I climbed out of the car with far less enthusiasm. The air was hot and muggy, and from all around came the whirring of cicadas. The sun was sinking to the west, adding a gold tinge to the light slanting through the trees. I peered at the house. Overgrown hedges hugged the walls, and vines of ivy covered half the brickwork. Patches of brown, dead grass dotted the lawn, and the garden plot that ran in front of the porch was choked with weeds.

A knot was slowly forming in my stomach. Until I saw the house, the impact of the move hadn't really hit me. We really *were* moving to a new town, starting a new life... leaving my old life behind. "I didn't even get to say goodbye to Phyllis," I whimpered.

My mom didn't seem to hear me. "The mayor was gracious enough to find us this place on short notice." She turned to me. "Lesley, aren't you hot in that jacket?"

"I'm fine," I grumbled, pulling my hood down lower.

My mother paused, then opened the car's trunk. "Here, I got you something." She held out a small box, as if my happiness could be bought with a present or something.

I lifted the lid from the box. Inside was a fancy, leather-bound journal with a clasp and lock, along with a matching brass key and a pen. I inserted the key into the lock and flipped through some of the blank pages. "I've never really kept a diary before."

"I did once," my mom explained, "back when I was having doubts about your father. Having something to confide in helped me see things more clearly." She smiled. "I think a diary will help you too. Just try it for a while, okay?"

I peered down at the journal, hugging it to my chest. Maybe my mom was right. Maybe this was what I needed to get through this mess.

* * *

That night, I had to sleep on an air mattress. Getting a moving truck to deliver to a place hidden inside magical wards was tricky, apparently. My mother said the rest of our furniture should arrive by the end of the week. But even after such a rough day, I couldn't sleep, so I took my mom's advice and tried to put my jumbled thoughts down on paper. Under the beam of a flashlight, I peered at the pages of my new diary, rereading what I'd just written. Some of the details—even though I'd just lived through them— seemed crazy. Would my diary end up sounding like the ravings of a lunatic?

On the floor next to me, my phone buzzed. My eyes widened as I peered at the glowing screen. It was a message from Phyllis.

You haven't been at school in two days. Is something wrong?

A lump lodged in my throat. I set my phone aside and curled up, hugging myself. How was I supposed to even respond? I wasn't normal. I wasn't going to be normal ever again.

* * *

I spent the rest of the week sulking. My mom tried her best to get me to explore the town—to visit the café down the street or to meet the mayor who had so kindly allowed us into Misty Hollow—but each time I refused. She was patient with me, but as the week wore on I could tell I was getting on her nerves.

By the end of it, though, I was starting to feel better. Well, maybe "better" wasn't the right word. It was more like I was finally resigned to my fate. Besides, I had to go to school eventually, and by the time Monday came, I was curious to see what kinds of fae would be my new classmates. From what I remembered of my mother's stories, Misty Hollow was home to all sorts of mythical creatures—except, as it turned out, they weren't just mythical after all.

The morning sky was hazy and smeared with wispy clouds. I peered through the window of my mom's car, frowning. In her stories, I'd imagined the school as a mysterious, enchanted castle. I was a little disappointed to see it was actually a squat brick building just like any other high school. A paved path ran up to the school's front steps, across a stretch of lawn dotted with a few trees. Further down the street, a row of school buses idled. Reluctantly, I opened the door.

"Have a good day, sweetie," my mom said. "You're sure you'll be all right riding the bus home? If you need me to come pick you up..."

"I'll be fine, Mom." I leaned over and gave her a one-armed hug. I stepped out of the car and adjusted the strap of my satchel—after what had happened to me, it was difficult to wear a backpack. I fidgeted with the hood of my jacket, making sure it still covered my forehead as I stepped through the front entrance.

My eyes widened. It would have been just like any other high school, except the students weren't human.

Many of them looked human enough at first glance, but then I would notice a tail or tusks or pointed ears. Among them, others with more obvious features stood out. A boy strode down the hall upon the four hooves of a horse. A girl rolled along in a wheelchair, her fins glistening as her fish-like tail swayed.

A mermaid. An actual mermaid! I glanced at the boy again. *And he's a centaur!* He gave me a funny look. I realized I was gaping at him and glanced away. I pulled out my phone and looked at the message with my locker number.

As I headed along the hall in search of my new locker, I passed by a pair of girls talking with each other. One of them had golden feathers instead of hair and feathery wings instead of arms. *A harpy,* I thought, recalling my mother's stories. The other girl had furry ears atop her head emerging from carrot-orange hair, as well as a bushy fox tail that swished behind her. *And she's a kitsune.*

The two girls noticed me, and the bird-girl pointed a stubby wing-claw. "That must be the new girl. I heard her mom used to live in Misty Hollow but that she ran away with a demon." The fox-girl's eyes widened, her ears swiveling in alarm. I bit my lip, trying to ignore them as I hurried past.

Further along, I yelped as a hunched, shaggy figure strode by me. His face—which was an elongated, wolf-like snout—seemed twisted into a frown, and his furry ears were laid back flat against his skull. He carried a backpack over one broad shoulder and didn't seem to notice me. *A werewolf!* The other day, my mom had reassured me werewolves weren't savage monsters like humans thought—at least not the ones in Misty Hollow. Still, I was a little creeped out.

A moment later, I noticed a girl watching me. Her eyes flickered strangely, as though they reflected the light of unseen candles. It was the same glow I'd seen in my mother's eyes a couple times since moving to Misty

Hollow—and even before that, I realized. It was the glow of witch-fire. *She's a witch too, then.*

The witch-girl gave me an exasperated look. "Hey, give the guy a break," she said, gesturing toward the werewolf. "He's probably just having a bad day."

"Sorry," I muttered. "I'm new here. I'm not used to—"

But she had already turned away. With a sigh, I looked at my phone again. Finally, I found the locker with the matching number. I unloaded some books from my satchel and set off in search of my homeroom.

A scraggly haired boy stepped in front of me, blocking my path. He had a pair of horns curving back from his temples, down and around his floppy ears. His legs were oddly bent, and cloven hooves emerged from the hems of his tattered jeans. *A satyr.*

"I heard there was a new girl in town." The goat-boy said, smirking. He stooped to peer underneath my hood. "Whatcha hiding under there?"

"None of your business!" I tugged at my hood as I hurried past him, but I should have watched where I was going because I bumped into someone.

Papers spilled from my satchel. The girl I'd bumped into spun to face me. Golden locks framed her face, hiding all but the tips of her pointed ears. Her eyes widened as she looked at me.

"Watch where you're going, freak," the elf-girl said, frowning. She stepped past me, ignoring the pile of papers on the floor.

Behind me, the goat-boy chuckled. A second later, I realized the hood of my jacket had slipped back. As fast as possible, I pulled it down over my forehead again. I glanced around, wondering who else had seen what was underneath.

As I kneeled to gather my things, my hand landed on top of someone else's. Someone had crouched next to me and was helping gather my spilled papers. I pulled my hand away from his.

"Uh, thanks," I murmured, accepting the stack of papers he offered me. I rose and turned to the boy who had helped me. His chestnut hair was perfectly combed, and a pair of bright, silver eyes peered through the lenses of his glasses. "I'm Lesley, by the way," I said, offering a hand.

His gaze flickered to the hood covering my forehead. A moment later, he shook my hand. "I'm Zack."

"Zack. Nice to meet you."

He offered me a smile. "I take it you're new in town?"

"Is it that obvious?"

He chuckled. "I'm actually new here as well. I just came to Misty Hollow a few weeks ago." Zack glanced around at the hallway. "I'm still getting used to everything, too."

"Really? That's so cool." I paused. "I mean, it's cool that you're also new here, not that you're still getting used to things."

He leaned in a bit closer, lowering his voice. "I saw what was under your hood. Can I ask—and I don't mean this in any negative way, but—what are you?"

I chewed my lip. "I'm a cambion—half human and half demon."

His brows rose. "Half… demon?"

My gaze sank downward. "Yeah."

Zack paused for a moment. "Well, I gotta get to homeroom." He turned to continue down the hall, but glanced back at me. "Nice meeting you, Lesley."

"Nice meeting you too, Zack." Once he had gone, I frowned. I couldn't tell if Zack had been frightened that I was part demon. I reached up to touch what was beneath my hood, then behind my back to inspect the knobby things hidden under my jacket, sprouting from between my shoulders.

3

The Fae

Sunlight streamed into the cafeteria, falling in rectangular patches across half the room. Students joined the lunch line or sat at the tables. Hooves clicked as a centaur worked his way through the crowd. A fairy fluttered her wings, hovering for a moment to peer past her classmates. A tusk-faced troll, his skin blue-gray like granite, ducked his head as he stepped through the entryway. It seemed like almost every kind of mythical creature I'd ever heard of attended the school. One, though, seemed to be missing. So far, I hadn't seen anyone who looked like me. I was beginning to worry no other cambions attended the school. What my mom had said about the mayor "allowing" us into Misty Hollow wasn't reassuring.

The seating arrangements had a pattern. The elves and fairies sat on the side toward the windows, in the half of the room bathed in sunlight, while every shaggy werewolf or glimmery-eyed witch or warlock seemed to be restricted to the other half of the room.

The blond elf-girl—the one I'd bumped into earlier that day—stepped through the entrance. If her fashionable jeans and matching denim jacket didn't give it away, her confident stride did. She was one of the popular girls, and she knew it. The elf headed for one of the tables on the light side and joined two other girls. One was a fairy with gossamer wings like those of a dragonfly. The other was a centaur, her coppery hair tied back in a ponytail that matched the actual horse tail swishing behind her.

"Hey, Nerissa," said the centaur, waving at the elf-girl.

"Pauline," the elf replied. She looked at the fairy. "Daphne."

"Riss." The fairy girl nodded.

The three girls noticed me watching. Pauline sized me up before crossing her arms. Daphne fluttered her wings, but followed Pauline's lead. Nerissa narrowed her eyes, shooting me a warning look. The message was clear: *You can't sit with us.*

Like I was going to let that stop me. I put on a smile and approached the table. "Hi." I offered the elf-girl a handshake. "Nerissa, is it? I'm Lesley. Sorry for bumping into you earlier."

"I'm sure you are," Nerissa said, rising from her seat. Pauline and Daphne glanced at one another before following her to a different table. I stood in stunned silence.

"Ouch," came a girl's voice from behind me. "Don't worry about her. Riss can be a huge jerk sometimes."

"Yeah, I noticed." I turned to face the girl, but when I did, I shivered.

Her skin was pale as porcelain. Wavy locks framed her face, reaching past her shoulders. Her hair was raven black except for a single white lock emerging above her forehead. But what had made me shiver was the pair of fangs glinting inside her mouth. *A vampire!* My mom had reassured me that, like werewolves, vampires weren't actually dangerous—not the ones from Misty Hollow, at least.

Still, I couldn't help but hesitate as I offered her a handshake. "Uh, I'm Lesley."

"I'm Sadie," the vampire replied. "I'd totally shake your hand, but..."

I blinked. "Oh, right. Vampires don't like sunlight, do they?" I stepped out of the patch of light and shook her hand. I shuddered a little—her skin was cold and clammy.

"You're the new cambion girl, right? You obviously don't know yet, but the light and dark fae tend to keep to themselves. I'm sure you can guess which of us are considered 'light' and which 'dark.'" Sadie pointed to one of the tables at the far side of the room. "Here, come sit with us." She smirked. "Don't worry, I don't bite."

Sadie seemed amused at my startled reaction. I cleared my throat. "So, um, vampires really are hurt by sunlight?"

She shrugged. "Sunlight is painful to us, but it doesn't, like, disintegrate us or anything like you see in the movies."

That was good to know. I'd hate to bump into her and have her turn into a pile of ash. I followed her to a table on the other side of the cafeteria. Two boys sat there, both of whom I recognized. One was the shaggy werewolf who had passed me in the hallway that morning. The other, to my surprise, was Zack.

Sadie sat across from them. "Everyone, this is Lesley." She gestured to the werewolf. "Lesley, this is Jeremy." She indicated the other boy. "And this is Zack. He's new in town, too."

I took a seat. "Actually, me and Zack have already met." I smiled at Zack before turning to the werewolf boy. "Um, hello."

He nodded at me and glanced away again.

"Jeremy has difficulty speaking when he's in werewolf form," Sadie explained. "Also, he gets kind of embarrassed whenever this happens to him. On the bright side, though, he says the cafeteria food seems way better when he's like this." Jeremy nodded again. "So, Lesley, you just got here?" Sadie asked.

"Yep," I said.

"I heard you came to town last week, but I haven't seen you at school until today."

I glanced away. "Well, I was sort of hiding at home all last week."

"It seems like you still are." Zack pointed to the hood draped over my brow.

Sadie sent him a look. "I'm sure she has her reasons. Remember what you told me earlier?"

"Oh, yeah, I totally get it." He looked at me. "Before I came here, I didn't know people like you—like us, I mean—actually existed, so I get what you're going through." He shook his head. "It feels weird to say 'us.' I'm still not used to thinking of myself as fae."

I peered at him. His ears were rounded, not pointed—he wasn't an elf. His teeth weren't sharpened into fangs—not a vampire either. He didn't seem to have any extra limbs or appendages. "Can I ask what kind of fae you are, Zack?"

He sighed. "I know I asked you that same thing earlier, Lesley, but... I'd rather not talk about it."

"Oh. Um, don't worry, it's cool. Forget I asked."

Sadie smiled at me. It might have seemed friendly if the expression hadn't also revealed her fangs. "Got any questions about this place?" she asked.

I glanced around the room. "Actually, yeah, I do. My mom said the fae are trying to go unnoticed, but... how can a place like this possibly remain secret? I mean, like, the Internet exists."

"Oh, everyone's way too careful to let anything suspicious get onto the Internet." Sadie took out her phone, scooted next to me, and snapped a selfie of the two of us. She posted the image to her Instagram page, typing *Second week of sophomore year, at lunch with my new friend :)* as the caption. "A picture like this doesn't reveal anything suspicious, so it's just fine. But if I were to, say, post a picture showing off my fangs, it would piss off everyone and probably get me in trouble because pictures like that can attract unwanted attention. There's nothing the fae hate more than humans wandering into town in search of ghosts or Bigfoot or whatever."

Even though I hardly knew her, I kind of liked that Sadie called me a friend. I glanced at the fangs poking from behind her lips, and they didn't seem quite as unnerving as before. "What about the magic wards?" I asked. "Don't they hide this place from outsiders?"

"The wards make Misty Hollow harder to find, but they won't stop humans from entering—there's not enough magic anymore for that kind of defense."

"That's what we get for relying too much on magic," Zack murmured.

I looked at him. "You don't like magic?"

"Oh, quite the opposite," he began, but before he could explain, his gaze was drawn past me. The sound of hooves clicked across the floor. Zack narrowed his eyes. "Oh, great, it's that guy again."

"Ugh," Sadie muttered. "That's Mercury," she said to me. "Also known as Murk the Jerk."

"Hey, new girl," came a sneering voice.

The goat-boy from earlier was standing behind my chair. Another boy stood next to him—an ogre, judging by his tusks.

"Leave her alone, Murk," Sadie warned.

Murk shrugged. "I can't help it, Sadie. I'm a satyr—it's in my nature to be mischievous." He turned to me and reached out. "My friend here is *really* curious to see what's under that hood of yours."

"Hey, don't touch me!" I tried to scoot away, but he and the ogre-boy each grabbed one of my sleeves and hauled me from my seat. "Stop it!" I cried, struggling against them.

Both Sadie and Jeremy jumped up from their seats. Jeremy bared his teeth with a growl while Sadie flashed her fangs. "Murk, let her go."

The satyr-boy ignored her. He and his ogre friend held me by my wrists as Murk unzipped my jacket. My eyes widened. "No! Please don't!"

Jeremy strode around the table, snarling menacingly. Before he could reach the two bullies, Murk flipped my hood back and pulled my jacket down past my waist. I fought against the boys' grip and broke free, but only managed to fall to the floor. As I clambered to my knees, astonished whispers surrounded me. Apparently, my classmates had never seen anything like me before.

I tried to reach back and pull my jacket up again, but it was too late. Everyone had seen. My tail lashed—slender and sinuous, covered in red skin and ending in an arrowhead-shaped barb. A pair of large, bat-like wings extended from between my shoulders, emerging through slits cut in the back of my shirt. And upon my brow was a pair of devil horns—two inches long, sleek and shiny like fingernails and red as blood.

I drew in my membranous wings, folding them against my back again. But I couldn't hide them—even when folded, the stubby, clawed thumbs hovered above my shoulders while the webbed fingers reached down to my waist. I looked up to find Jeremy standing snout to nose with Murk. But the thing that put fear into the bully's expression—and briefly brought the whole cafeteria to silence—was Zack.

"Leave her alone!" he cried as he shoved his way past Jeremy and got right in Murk's face.

I gasped—Zack's eyes shone with the flickering reflection of a hundred candles—the glow of witch-fire.

Murk's eyes widened. "Whoa," he said, backing away a step. "I, uh, I didn't know you were a..." A second later, he and his friend scurried back to their own table.

Zack let out a breath.

I blinked at him. "You're a warlock!"

A flicker of witch-fire lingered in his eyes as he glanced at me. "Yeah, but like I said, I'd rather not talk about it."

* * *

The first day of school seemed to last forever, but somehow I made it to the end. I trudged out through the entrance, joining the crowd of students as they headed toward the buses parked along the street. Leaves rustled in the breeze, and the afternoon sun shone among a patchwork of clouds. In spite of the warm afternoon, I was wrapped up in my jacket, my wings flat against my back and my tail coiled around my waist, my horns concealed beneath the jacket's hood.

I took a seat on one of the buses and stared out the window, trying to ignore the students whispering about me. Thankfully, it wasn't long before the bus came to my neighborhood and I got off. Once the bus rolled away down the street, I slipped off my jacket and allowed my wings to unfurl. I wiped the sweat from my brow—from between my devil horns—and stretched my wings, spreading them to their full span. I frowned at my shadow on the sidewalk.

The sunlight seeping through the membranes revealed the bones inside, which resembled a pair of huge, distorted hands.

I folded my wings again and glanced down at the jacket bundled under my arm. *Is there any point in hiding now? Everyone has already seen.*

I arrived at the small brick house that had become my new home. My mother's car was parked in the driveway beneath the shade of the trees. The weeds had been cleared out of the garden plot below the porch, and the hedges were neatly trimmed. Past the side of the house came the sound of a spade digging into the soil. I peeked around the corner and saw my mom kneeling there, pulling up more weeds. I chewed my lip before quietly turning the other direction, sneaking around the opposite side of the house.

The back yard was sunnier than the front, with only a couple of trees at the far corners. Unopened bags of mulch were stacked along the fence to one side, and the locations of future garden plots were marked with lengths of string staked into the ground. A small patio connected to the back of the house, its concrete cracked and weathered. In the far corner of the yard, a willow tree stood guard over an old wooden shed. I crept across the lawn and brushed aside some hanging willow branches. I pulled the latch, and the shed's door creaked open—it was unlocked, just like I'd hoped.

Dust drifted in the sunlight streaming through the shed's lone window. Garden tools were arranged along one wall, and along the other was a workbench strewn with all sorts of things. Bottles and jars were filled with oils and salts, bundles of herbs, a collection of colorful crystals, even a few animal bones. In the midst of everything was an old handwritten notebook—my mother's spellbook. These were the tools my mom used to practice witchcraft—to make magic. Somehow, she'd kept this a secret for my entire life, and I'd never even suspected. Until now, I hadn't really believed my mom's herbal remedies—or rather, potions, as I now knew—were why I hardly got sick or why my cuts and bruises always seemed to heal so quickly.

At the far end of the room stood a tall bookcase. Dust and grime covered the glass panes of the bookcase doors, and a heavy chain with a padlock was threaded through the handles. Old books and other random items sat on the shelves inside the case. My mom hadn't told me what the bookcase was for, but she'd left the padlock in place during the move and had seemed very concerned that the movers not jostle the bookcase as they'd unloaded it from the truck. I got the sense it was where she locked away dangerous magical objects.

I drew in a breath, inhaling the mingled scent of herbs and earth and dust. My frustration from school melted away, replaced by a feeling of calm. I couldn't explain why, but this place was comforting.

The shed door opened behind me. "Lesley," my mother said, "what are you doing in here?" I turned. My mom stood in the doorway, her hands on her hips. She tossed the spade she was holding into a bin, then removed her gardening gloves and threw them in as well. Witch-fire flickered in her eyes. "I told you to stay out of my workshop."

"Mom," I stammered, "I just wanted to see what's in here."

"So you decided to sneak in?" She grabbed my wrist and dragged me back out into the yard.

Her anger faded quickly, though. She turned to me with a regretful look. "I'm sorry for yelling at you. It's just... the stuff in there can be dangerous." She laid a gentle hand on my shoulder. "Promise me you'll stay out of there?"

"Yes, Mother," I muttered.

"So... how was school?" my mom asked.

"It was awful! Some jerks pulled my jacket off during lunch, and everyone saw my horns and wings."

"Oh, Lesley. You don't need to be ashamed."

"Well, I *am* ashamed, okay? I used to have nightmares about demons, remember? Now I find out I'm *related* to them, and I'm supposed to just be okay with that?" I sat on a stack of mulch bags, hiding my face in my hands.

My mom sat next to me, wrapping an arm around my shoulder. I leaned against her, biting my lip until I could contain the moisture in my eyes.

Finally, I looked up at her. "You still haven't told me anything about my father."

My mother blinked in surprise. "You really want to know about him?" I nodded. "All right," she continued. "He was an incubus named Caelum."

"What's an incubus?"

"A tempter demon. The incubi and succubi serve the princes of Hell as tempters and temptresses. Their job is to seduce humans."

"But aren't demons, like, ugly? They have horns and hooves and red skin, don't they?"

"Only in their true form. Incubi and succubi can shapeshift to appear human." Her gaze slid past me into the distance. "Your father was quite handsome."

"Did you... love him?" I asked.

She sighed. "When I first met Caelum, I wasn't much older than you are now. Who knows if what I felt was really love?"

"But then why did you leave him?"

My mother chewed her lip. "It wasn't because of him. It was because of his master, Asmodeus."

I could tell there was more to the story but that she didn't want to talk about it, so I changed the subject. "After what happened at lunch today, everyone was gawking like they'd never seen anything like me before. I'm starting to think I'm the only cambion in town."

"Cambions aren't the most common type of fae." She looked at me sadly. "And... well, since demons aren't welcome in the havens, cambions usually aren't either. The mayor made an exception in your case."

I sighed. "That explains all the funny looks I was getting."

She gave me a hug. "I'm sorry you have to go through all this. But being a cambion isn't all bad."

"What do you mean?"

She smiled. "You have wings, silly. You can fly!" My mom rose and extended her hand toward the shed, murmuring an incantation. An old-fashioned broomstick, made from twigs tied around a gnarled stick, flew out through the shed door. She caught the floating broomstick and turned to me. "If you want to try, I'll stay right beside you."

I blinked. After everything else, why was I surprised to learn that witches really did fly on broomsticks? My mom was inviting me to come *fly* with her. I peered over my shoulder, slowly unfurling one of my wings. "I can really fly with these things?"

"Of course you can, sweetie."

My heart thumped—maybe from excitement, maybe from fear. "But... I don't know how."

"It should come instinctively. Cambions can fly as soon as their wings emerge." My mother straddled the broom like it was a bicycle and gave me an encouraging nod.

I trembled, feeling as nervous as when I'd first learned to ride a bike without training wheels. Even though it was nearly ten years ago, I still remembered that day clearly—my mom on her bike next to mine, smiling encouragingly as I gripped my handlebars with white knuckles. I felt like I was reliving that day, except now my mom wasn't on a bike but a broomstick, and I had nothing to hold me up at all. Even so, I tried flapping my wings a couple of times. They seemed so strong. Maybe I really could fly. I faced the far end of the yard, trying to judge the distance to the house. Something told me I would need a running start.

But my legs were shaking. "No," I stammered. "I can't do this!" Turning, I dashed inside the house and shoved my way through my bedroom door. I collapsed onto my bed, hugging myself as I struggled to hold back tears. It wasn't the thought of flying that had scared me. As I'd felt the strength of my wings, it had become clear that they were a part of me—not just some abnormal growth, but truly a part of me.

4

The Wellspring

If my second day at Misty Hollow High School was as stressful as the first one, I didn't think I would survive the semester.

I stood at my locker, frowning up at the hood draped over my brow. Underneath my jacket, my wings were folded flat against my back, my tail coiled around my waist like a belt. Earlier that day, I'd overheard some of my classmates whispering about me. Hiding my demonic features wasn't making things any better.

I glanced at the other students shuffling along the hallway. No one else was embarrassed about their strange attributes. No one else tried to hide them. *They'd better get used to mine too,* I decided. Before I could chicken out, I slipped off my jacket and shoved it in my locker. I let my wings unfurl partway and my tail hang down behind me. Taking a breath, I marched down the hall to my next class. I entered the classroom and headed for a desk in the back row—not because I was afraid to be seen, I told myself, but so my wings wouldn't block anyone's view.

Among the dozen students seated at the desks was the snooty elf-girl, Nerissa. I pretended I didn't notice her. But she must have noticed me because she gasped.

"Did someone steal your jacket?" she asked with a sneer.

I hesitated, then faced her. "No." I crossed my arms, spreading my wings and curling my tail to the side in a way I hoped looked menacing. "I've decided you're just gonna have to get used to me." I was pleased when her eyes widened just a little.

Not long after I'd taken a seat, a shaggy werewolf hurried in. His elongated legs barely fit under his desk, but he managed to squeeze himself in just before the bell rang.

Nerissa smirked at him. "Aw, having a bad day again, Jeremy?"

He growled at her.

"Leave him alone, Riss," I said.

Nerissa shot a glare at me. "No one asked your opinion, freak."

The history teacher, Mrs. Osborn, strode in. Her wiry, silver hair was tied back in a bun, revealing pointed elf ears jutting from the sides of her head. "Good morning, class." Her gaze lingered warily on me a moment as she took attendance. "As we were discussing yesterday," the teacher continued, "the fae were once divided into two factions—the Seelie and the Unseelie." She peered over the half-moon lenses of her glasses. "Who can tell me why this was so?"

Nerissa raised her hand. "They had different views of mankind. Some fae strove to coexist peacefully with humans. They were called 'light' and 'blessed' and became known as the Seelie. But others saw humans as a threat. They came to be known as 'dark' and 'unholy' and were called Unseelie."

I couldn't help but notice how Nerissa glanced at Jeremy, then at me, as she explained the Unseelie. I squeezed the pencil I was holding.

Mrs. Osborn nodded. "That's exactly right, Nerissa. The Seelie saw humans as friends and allies, but the Unseelie viewed them as enemies."

My fist clenched tighter, and I raised my hand.

"Yes, Miss..." The teacher consulted the class roster. "Miss Lesley Robinson?"

"My mom explained it to me differently. Humans saw some fae as beautiful, but others as ugly or frightening. They befriended some but shunned and vilified others just because of their appearance. It was the humans who made friends or enemies with the Seelie and the Unseelie, not the other way around."

"That's... an interesting theory," Mrs. Osborn said slowly. "But let us move on. Class, who can tell me what caused the two factions to unite?" The teacher's gaze slid past me. "Jeremy, do you know the answer?"

His fur bristled as he stared blankly at Mrs. Osborn.

She narrowed her eyes at him. "Please answer the question."

"Mrs. Osborn," I said, "he has trouble speaking when—"

She ignored me. "Answer the question, Jeremy," the teacher repeated.

The wolf-boy glanced nervously at his classmates and huffed in a breath. A low, guttural growl emerged from his throat, and I could barely understand his words. "The... ebbing... of... magic."

"Yes, Jeremy, the ebbing of magic. As the wellsprings began to dry up, we fae had less and less access to magic and became less able to protect our lands from human encroachment. In the end, we were forced to retreat to havens such as this one, close to the remaining wellsprings. The Seelie did not forget their brethren, of course, and allowed the Unseelie to—yes, Lesley?"

I lowered my straining arm. "I was told the Seelie and Unseelie came together as equals. Out of necessity, they were forced to set aside notions of 'light' and 'dark.'"

"Lesley Robinson, you appear to be confused about which of us is the teacher and which is the student." She glared at me over gleaming half-moon lenses, unblinking.

I lowered my gaze and spent the rest of class doodling in my notebook, ignoring the lecture. Finally, the bell rang. I kept my gaze on the floor as I shuffled into the hallway.

I meandered along, vaguely heading toward my locker, when I heard Zack yelp. My brows rose, and I picked up my pace. Zack had his back against the wall, Murk looming over him. The goat-boy held something up in his hand, out of Zack's reach.

"Hey, give those back!" Zack said.

"You made me look like a fool yesterday." Murk lifted the thing he was holding—Zack's glasses. "I didn't know you don't actually have any powers." With his free hand, Murk shoved Zack into the lockers. "You really are powerless, aren't you?"

Zack found his balance again. He squinted up at Murk. "I didn't mean to make you look bad. I just got angry, okay? Please give me back my glasses."

It's not fair. Zack didn't deserve to be treated like that. He was just as bewildered at this place as I was, yet in spite of that, he had been kind to me. "Stop it, Murk!" I shoved my way between Zack and the satyr. For good measure, I flared my wings and let my tail lash from side to side like an angry cat's.

Murk blinked at me in surprise. "All right, new girl. Since you asked so nicely..." He let go of the glasses, letting them clatter to the floor. Murk snickered as he disappeared into the crowd.

Zack knelt down, feeling his way across the floor. I picked up his glasses and handed them to him. He squinted through the lenses and polished them on his shirt before fitting the frames to his face. "Thanks Lesley."

My heart thumped. Until that moment, I hadn't appreciated just how lucky I was to have met Zack. We were both going through the same struggles, and it was *so* nice not to have to face those struggles alone. Also... how had I not noticed just how striking his silver eyes were?

"Uh, just returning the favor." I paused. "You know, um, I'm really glad to not be the only new person in town."

Zack smiled at me. He had such nice white teeth, brilliant like his eyes. "I feel the same way, Lesley." He tilted his head. "You're not wearing your jacket today?"

I shrugged. "No one else is hiding their creature features."

He regarded me for a moment. "This may take some getting used to."

I looked away to hide my disappointment. *Does he think I'm ugly like this?* I changed the subject. "Is it true what Murk was saying about you not having powers?"

"Not exactly," Zack said. "I'm not completely powerless. I just really suck at witchcraft. I can hardly get simple spells to work, and forget about more complicated ones."

I faced him again. "I've seen my mom do some amazing things with magic. I'd probably be super frustrated if I was in your situation."

"Actually, it's likely you've inherited some magical ability from her. Not to mention your demon father... demons are supposed to have *really* powerful magic. Maybe you do too."

I shivered. "How would I know if I did?"

"If you have the ability, you'll just sort of feel the presence of magic."

"Really? What does it feel like?"

"It's kind of hard to describe." He paused. "Your mom hasn't mentioned anything about this?"

"No, she hasn't." I frowned. If I did have magical abilities, why wouldn't she tell me?

* * *

I approached a door beneath a sign that said *Principal's Office*. A row of chairs lined one side of the hallway. A few of my classmates, including Sadie and Jeremy, sat in the chairs or leaned against the wall, waiting. The hallway was silent except for the ticking of a clock on the wall.

I stilled my twitching tail and sat down in one of the chairs, glancing at the others. "You guys were called here too? Are we in trouble or something?"

Sadie gave me a smile—which, despite her fangs, didn't seem all that unsettling. "No, we're not in trouble. The principal just likes to keep tabs on certain students."

I peered at the others again. Besides Sadie and Jeremy, there were two warlocks, a vampire boy, and a girl who was also a werewolf, although at the moment she was in human form. All of them—all of *us*—were Unseelie. "Certain *kinds* of students, I think you mean."

Sadie leaned closer. "It really isn't fair. There are stereotypes about the fae, but they're not true. Look at me, for example. As a vampire, I'm supposed to be all dour and brooding, but do I seem like that?"

"Not really," I replied. "What about me? What are cambions supposed to be like?"

She paused. "Well, demons are supposed to be pure evil, so... that, probably."

"Pure evil…" Behind my back, my wings drooped.

The office door opened, and the blue-gray troll emerged, ducking down to fit through. With a few rumbling words, he told Sadie she was up next. Sadie stepped into the office, and I craned my neck to listen. Sadie spoke in flattering tones, and a woman's voice replied with approval. Before long, the vampire girl emerged again and told one of the warlocks it was his turn.

Sadie whispered to me as she passed, "Principal Constance likes to play mind games. Don't let her get to you."

I waited as one by one the other students faced the principal. Finally, Jeremy was called in. It sounded like the principal was unhappy he had "lost control" again. After enduring some scolding, Jeremy emerged from the office, his wolf ears laid back flat, his gaze on the floor. He grunted at me, jerking a clawed thumb over his shoulder, and shuffled away down the hall.

I rose from my chair, carefully tucking my wings against my back, and peeked through the door. "Principal Constance?"

"Come in," said the principal. She was a tall, narrow-faced woman who looked about the same age as my mother. Elf ears swept up through her auburn hair, their pointed, curving shape reminding me of daggers. The woman set aside some papers she had been shuffling through. "Miss Lesley Robinson?"

"Yes, ma'am."

She pointed to the pair of chairs facing the desk. "Please, sit." I obeyed. "So you're Jane Robinson's daughter?"

"I am, yes."

"I used to know Jane. We both attended school here, in fact. She caused quite a scandal when she ran off with that incubus."

I crossed my arms. "Is there a reason you called me here?"

She rose from her chair, her high heels clicking across the floor as she approached. "As you no doubt have noticed, some of the students at my school have certain attributes that could be dangerous. I must see that those students do not pose a threat to the others."

"You mean like how the fairies can cause all sorts of mischief with their magic or how the centaurs can kick people really hard?"

She narrowed her eyes but otherwise kept her expression smooth. "I've never seen a cambion before. Is it true you have claws on your wings?"

I hesitated. "Well... yeah."

"Let me see."

I shifted in the chair and unfurled one of my wings. Principal Constance frowned at the webbed appendage. "Your claws, are they very sharp?"

"Um, I guess so."

"And your horns and the barb at the end of your tail, those are sharp as well?"

"Yes," I admitted.

She leaned down, looking me in the eye. "But these... unique features of yours, they won't pose a danger to your classmates, will they?"

"Of course not. I would never hurt anyone."

The principal regarded me for a long moment. "Very well, Miss Robinson." She waved a hand toward the door. "You may go now."

* * *

After a week at such an unusual school, the weekend couldn't come soon enough. There were some woods past the edge of my neighborhood, just a couple blocks from the house, and I'd been meaning to go exploring. On Friday evening, I finally got the chance.

Dry leaves crunched beneath my shoes. Shafts of amber light slanted through the branches, casting dappled patterns on the trail. The whirring of the cicadas in the trees was quieting down as crickets and katydids began their evening chorus. A sense of calm washed over me as I breathed in the warm, fresh air.

Something was visible along the trail ahead. It turned out to be the ruins of an old, burned down cabin. All that remained was a crumbling chimney standing above a patch of stone floor. I explored the clearing for a bit before heading deeper into the forest.

After following the winding trail for a while, I realized it was getting late and that I should head back. I turned and retraced my steps, but the path didn't seem familiar. Twenty minutes later, I was certain I should have passed the old cabin, but it was nowhere in sight, and the forest was getting dark. I tried not to panic as I peered this way and that into the fading twilight.

A light in the distance bobbed up and down like someone carrying a lantern. "Hey!" I ran after the light, stepping off the path. "Wait up!" Whoever it was didn't seem to hear me because the light kept receding into the distance.

"Stop!" a voice called out. I turned, and a red-haired woman stepped out of the trees. She was dressed in a park ranger's uniform. Her cowboy hat was pulled conspicuously low, covering the tops of her ears. In her hand, she grasped what appeared to be a wooden walking stick. "Follow me," she said.

The woman led me back to the trail and faced me with a stern look. "That was a will-o'-the-wisp. They like to lead travelers in the wrong direction. Do *not* follow them." She narrowed her eyes at me. "And you shouldn't be out here unsupervised."

"Sorry," I muttered. "Um, where am I, exactly?"

The woman removed her hat, revealing a pair of pointed elf ears. "You're in the Sacred Grove."

I blinked—the term sounded familiar, like it was from one of my mom's stories, but I couldn't remember.

"Didn't they teach you anything in school?" she asked.

"Sorry... I'm kind of new to all of this."

The woman sighed. "Which haven are you from?"

Which haven? How lost did I get? "Misty Hollow," I answered.

She turned. "This way."

I followed her along a trail which, again, seemed different from before. She glanced back at me. "You shouldn't be out here without a disguise, either. Humans sometimes get lost in here. What if one of them saw you?"

"I'm sorry," I muttered. *Wouldn't want any humans to see a freak like me, now would we?* I noticed a row of runic symbols carved down the length of her walking stick. "You're a dryad, aren't you? One of the forest guardians."

"Oh, so you do know something, after all."

I ignored her sarcastic tone. "My mom once told me a story about the Sacred Grove, but I don't remember the details."

"This is the grove of Yggdrasil."

That name sounded more familiar. "Yggdrasil... the World Tree?"

"Yes. Its roots reach out to drink from the wellsprings, including the one at Misty Hollow. The roots knit together otherwise distant places, forming the Sacred Grove."

"Oh, now I remember. The Sacred Grove exists in many places at once... somehow. It connects all the fae havens."

"Yes, but the paths are ever shifting, so it's easy to get lost." She gave me an impatient look. "Now, do you want to get home, or will you keep asking questions?"

I remained silent as I followed her through the dusk. Before long, we emerged into the clearing with the burned out cabin. "Do you know where you are now?" the dryad asked.

"Yes... thank you."

"Unless you want to get lost again, don't come past here." With a twirl of her staff and a rustling of leaves, the dryad vanished back into the forest. I blinked at the spot where she had been standing—she'd disappeared so quickly, I thought she must have used magic. Even though I'd seen my mother cast a few spells already, witnessing magic still gave me shivers. I took a breath and turned toward home. Once again, a sense of calm washed over me. It was the same feeling I got when I'd sneaked into my mother's workshop.

I stopped mid-stride. The wellspring—Misty Hollow's source of magic. My thoughts traced back to something Zack had said earlier that week, about how, if I had magical abilities, I would feel the presence of magic. *This calming feeling,* I wondered as I strolled through the twilight, *is this what magic feels like?*

* * *

I was hopeful my second week in Misty Hollow would be better than the first. But neither me nor my mother realized we weren't as safe inside the magic wards as we'd thought.

I approached what had become my usual table in the school cafeteria. Zack was there, along with a boy I'd never seen before. The new boy was short and lanky, with shaggy hair in need of a haircut. I sat down at the table. "Hi, I'm—" I looked more closely at the boy. "Wait... Jeremy?"

He gave me an awkward smile. "You haven't seen me in my human form yet, have you?"

"No, I guess I haven't."

The school bell rang. Jeremy peered past me, snickering. I followed his gaze to the cafeteria entrance. Sadie stood there, directly underneath the P.A. speaker. Her hands were clapped over her ears. She lowered her hands and frowned at the device on the wall.

"That was *not* something to laugh at, Jeremy," Sadie grumbled, striding over to our table. "We vampires have *very* sensitive hearing." She plopped down on one of the seats, set her lunch bag on the table, and took out a thermos full of—well, it should be obvious what was in her thermos.

I cleared my throat. "So, Zack, how are you doing today?"

"Okay, I guess," Zack murmured.

"What's wrong?"

Zack glanced at me, then at Jeremy and Sadie. "I think I'm finally ready to talk about why I came to Misty Hollow. Is it okay if I tell you?"

"Of course," Sadie said. "We're your friends." Jeremy and I nodded along with her.

Zack took a breath. "When my parents found out I was a warlock, they kicked me out. You know that one Bible verse? 'Thou shalt not suffer a witch to live.' I guess I should be grateful all they did was disown me. Anyway, I tried calling them over the weekend, but they still don't want to talk to me."

I gaped. "Your parents kicked you out? That's awful!"

He sighed. "Fortunately, I was able to get in touch with one of the warlocks here in town, and he was kind enough to take me in. I've been staying with him and his family for the past few weeks."

"So you were born to ordinary human parents?" Sadie asked.

Zack nodded. "Apparently it's uncommon, but it does happen sometimes."

Sadie smiled gently. "Well, even if your parents are ashamed, it doesn't mean you need to be too."

He shook his head. "It's not that I'm ashamed. It's more about how unfair it is that I have to put up with stuff like that even though, without witchcraft, I'm basically just a human."

"I totally get it," I said. "How do you think I feel about having the universal symbol of evil growing out of my forehead?" I peered into his eyes. "If you ever need someone to talk to, just let me know."

Zack blinked, and his mood seemed to lighten. "Thanks, Lesley."

I smiled back at him. "Um, also, I wanted to ask you something. You said magic has a certain feeling to it. Is it, like, an inexplicable sense of calm?"

He nodded. "Yeah, kind of."

"I felt something like that over the weekend when I was exploring the woods past the edge of my neighborhood. That's where the town's wellspring is, isn't it? Could it be magic I felt there?"

"Those woods are overflowing with magic. Yeah, that *is* probably was what you felt." He grinned at me. "That would be amazing if you turned out to have magical abilities."

"Yeah," Jeremy snickered. "You could set Murk's pants on fire with a snap of your fingers. That would shut him up for sure."

I regarded him for a moment. "I'll tell you what I'd do. Jeremy, you *look* human right now. Sadie, all you need to do to appear human is not smile and avoid sunlight. And Zack, no one would suspect you're a warlock except for when your eyes glow. But me, I'm stuck looking like this twenty-four-seven."

"Lesley—" Sadie began.

I shook my head. "You don't understand. I used to have nightmares about demons. Even now, demons *still* freak me out. Just dealing with the fact I'm part demon is bad enough. But the worst part is I'm stuck here. I can never leave Misty Hollow, not while looking like this. It's *so* unfair that I can never go back to the human world, that I'll never see my best friend Phyllis again." I sniffed and brushed at one of my eyes. "If I had magic, I would use it to, like, shapeshift or something. I'd use my magic to return to human form, to hide these horrible horns and tail and wings."

5

The Amulet

I lay sprawled on my bed, reading a book. The lamp on my nightstand filled my bedroom with a gentle glow. Between the slats of the window blinds, the sky was fading from deep crimson to the velvety blue of night.

I jumped at the sound of a knock at the front door. Crinkling my brow, I set aside my book and stepped into the hallway. I wasn't expecting anyone, and since moving to Misty Hollow, we'd never gotten visitors.

Rugby was in the foyer, his ears back, his fur bristling as he growled at the door. "Rugby!" I chided the dog, pushing him aside. I jumped again at more impatient knocking. Hurriedly, I switched on the lamp on an end table and opened the door. A man stood on the front porch, dressed in an old-fashioned suit and a top hat, grasping a gentleman's cane in one hand. A perfectly trimmed goatee and mustache encircled his mouth. He smiled at me, but something in that expression was unnerving.

Rugby barked viciously. The man shot a single glance at the dog, which was all it took to make Rugby skitter away down the hall, whimpering in terror.

The man turned back to me. "Hello, Lesley. Is your mother here? I wish to speak with her."

My tail was swishing, and my wings were half-spread. How did he know my name? I swallowed and turned. "Mom?" I called out.

As the seconds ticked by, the man's polite smile slipped. His cane clicked across the floor as he stepped inside, uninvited. He reached up and removed his top hat, revealing the shiny, smooth skin of his perfectly bald head. He let go, and the hat vanished in a swirl of smoke and flames. He looked at me and seemed to remember once more to hide his annoyance behind that fake smile of his.

Moments later, footsteps came down the hallway toward me. "Lesley," my mother said, "get away from him!" Brandishing her magic wand, she stepped between me and the man. "You're not welcome here, Asmodeus."

The man's smile vanished, but he didn't seem frightened at all. Instead, he looked angry. He twirled his fingers, and the wand shot out of my mother's grasp, clattering away down the hallway. He made another gesture, and my mother flew back, slamming against the wall. Her feet dangled inches from the floor—some invisible force pinned her there.

"Mom!" I leaped forward, but Asmodeus gestured toward me. A strange, cloying force coiled around my wrists and ankles. I yelped as I was dragged down to my knees. More invisible forces wrapped themselves around my jaw, holding my mouth shut.

Asmodeus turned back to my mother. He grasped her by the chin, forcing her to meet his gaze. "Did you really think you could hide here, Jane? Did you think this town's pitiful wards could conceal you from me?"

"I'm only a witch now," my mother said. "I don't practice sorcery anymore. I'm no longer of any interest to you."

"But the contract you signed is still binding. You remember what it said, don't you?" His gaze turned toward me.

"No!" she cried, struggling against the invisible bonds. "I won't let you take her!"

Asmodeus shook his head. "It was too late by the time you tried to suppress your daughter's transformation. Your dear Caelum had already felt her power awakening. Lesley will become my servant, just as we agreed."

My insides squirmed. I wanted to scream, but invisible forces held my jaw shut tight. The man turned, kneeling to look at me. "What a fine specimen you are. And what's this... you've tiny little horns upon your brow? Adorable!" I flinched away as he reached out to touch my face.

"Stop!" my mother cried. "Leave her alone!"

In an instant, Asmodeus was on his feet again, face to face with her—it seemed impossible he could have moved so fast. He had raised one hand, as if about to slap her across the face, but he slowly lowered his arm. "It would be wise of you," he seethed, "to show a measure of humility in my presence."

She scowled and spat in his face. "Go to hell."

He blinked at her, then laughed. "Is that a joke? I see you haven't changed at all, Jane." He took a handkerchief and wiped the spit from his face. "Tell you what... I'll make a wager with you. Interested?"

She glared at him, but her expression softened as she looked toward me. "What kind of wager?" Asmodeus wiggled his fingers. My mother slid down from the wall, staggering to keep her balance. She looked at him again. "What kind of wager, Asmodeus?"

He flourished his hands like a showman. "Let us have Lesley choose freely for herself. If she chooses to join me before midnight on the winter solstice, you will let her go uncontested."

My mother glanced nervously between me and Asmodeus. "And if she doesn't?"

"Then I will free you from your contract and never trouble you again. You will forever be able to boast that you made a prince of Hell go slinking back to his brothers in shame." He twirled his fingers, and something appeared amid a swirl of flame—a writing quill and a parchment. He snatched them out of the air and held them out to my mother. "What do you say, Jane? Do we have a deal?"

"As if you're giving me a choice." My mother looked at me. She hesitated, but took the scroll and the quill. "Fine, I'll play your little game." She scribbled her signature on the scroll and shoved the quill and parchment at Asmodeus. "There, are you satisfied?"

He smiled as he took the scroll and placed it inside his jacket. "A pleasure doing business." He wiggled his fingers at me, and the invisible forces entwining me vanished. Asmodeus reached above his head as if to grasp something, and his top hat reappeared amid a swirl of smoke. He put on the hat and turned to go back outside. But as he closed the door, his gaze fell on me again. For an instant, fire glowed in his eyes, seething inside his pupils like hot coals.

I was trembling. I rose to my feet and ran over to my mother, wrapping my arms around her. She hugged me back. "Oh, sweetie!"

After a long moment, I slipped out of her embrace. "Mom," I whimpered. "I don't understand. What is going on? Who is Asmodeus?"

She placed a hand on my shoulder, leading me into the kitchen, and we sat down at the table. "Asmodeus is the chief prince of Hell."

"You mean he's... the devil?" I swallowed. "You *literally* made a deal with the devil?"

Her gaze sank to the tabletop, unable to meet mine. "In exchange for learning sorcery, I agreed to conceive a cambion child, which I was to give to Asmodeus to be his servant. But after you were born, when the demons came to take you..." Her gaze grew distant. "The way you cried and screamed as they held you... I couldn't bear the thought of you being taken away. I rescued you, and ever since, I've been trying to keep you hidden from Asmodeus."

"The nightmares..." My breath stuck in my throat. "The nightmares I used to have, they were actually *memories*!"

"I always thought so, yes. If only I'd taken you sooner, before the demons arrived..." My mother sniffed and wiped her eyes. "Lesley, I'm *so* sorry! I love you, and I regret ever thinking I could give you away like that." She hid her face in her hands as she collapsed into sobs.

"Mom, it's okay." I stepped around the table and hugged her. "It's okay. Asmodeus didn't get me, and he's not going to." She looked up at me, her eyes red with tears. I tried to smile, like what had just happened was no big deal. "I mean, why would he think I'd agree to serve him, anyway?"

She bit her lip, remaining silent.

"Well, I won't, that's for sure," I continued. "Do you think once we convince him of that, he'll really leave us alone?"

My mother sighed. "I don't know. But I promise, sweetie, I will do everything I can to keep you safe."

* * *

The final bell of the day echoed through the halls. Around me, the other students rose from their desks. I remained seated a little longer, slowly loading my satchel as I waited for my classmates to shuffle out the door. Once everyone else had gone, I got up and spread my wings, gently flapping them a few times. After keeping them folded against my back all day, they were getting cramped. My tail swayed listlessly as I stepped into the hallway. I followed the crowd as they funneled through the school's main entrance, out into the gray light of a cold, cloudy day. But as I headed down the front steps, a sight almost made me trip. A man in a suit and top hat stood by the edge of the pathway. Asmodeus was waiting for me.

I squared my shoulders, trying to ignore him as I passed by. But even though I didn't want it to—even though I was terrified—my gaze was drawn to his. Once again, that fire glowed within his eyes.

None of my classmates seemed to notice him. Only then did I realize I had stopped walking. I tried to turn away, but my legs felt heavy, my feet stuck to the pavement. Asmodeus approached, his lips twisted in a bemused smirk.

I swallowed. "What do you want, Asmodeus?"

He leaned forward conspiratorially. "I thought you'd like to know. Your mother, she has been lying to you."

I narrowed my eyes. "No, she hasn't."

"Like how she didn't hide from you the fact that you're half demon? Your mother never told you about your magical abilities either, did she?" My eyes widened, and his smile grew broader. "You already suspect, don't you? You've felt the presence of magic."

A shiver crawled through me.

"She doesn't want you to know about the power you've inherited," Asmodeus continued. "Tell me, does your mother forbid you from entering her workshop, where she keeps all her ingredients for witchcraft?" I shifted my gaze. "I thought so. She doesn't want you to feel the presence of

51

the magic there. She doesn't want you to recognize the ability you have. She is *lying* to you!"

"No, Asmodeus, *you're* the one who's lying!"

"Am I? Shall we put it to a test, then?" From inside his jacket, he pulled out something that glittered—a gold necklace. A blood red jewel hung from the chain, gleaming despite the gray light from the overcast sky. "This amulet is enchanted—infused with magical power. If you lack the talent, you will feel nothing from it at all. But if you *do* have it, you will feel the amulet's power and will be able to use it."

I tried to back away, but my feet were still rooted to the ground. Against my will, my hand extended, pulled by invisible forces. Asmodeus took a tattered parchment, pressing it into my open palm along with the necklace, and closed my hand around them. "The scroll contains a sampling of basic spells. Try to cast them. See that they work. Feel the power the amulet contains. When you want to learn more, the final spell will let you summon one of my servants. He will provide you with further guidance."

My skin crawled beneath his touch. "Is this supposed to tempt me into becoming your slave? It won't work!"

"My slave?" He laughed. "You will be no mere slave, Lesley. You will attend the Scholomance and be trained in the ways of sorcery." Asmodeus leaned in closer. "The Scholomance is the finest magic school in all the world, where the greatest of sorcerers are trained. I dare say you will fit in there much better than in this wretched place."

"Sorry, not interested."

"Not even a little? Not even if I told you that one of the spells you will learn is how to appear human again?"

My voice quavered. "What?"

"The spell is called transfiguration. It allows the servants of Hell to pass among humans unnoticed. With it, you will be able to hide your wings and tail and horns any time you wish and go back to looking like an ordinary human girl."

I hesitated, then narrowed my eyes. "No! Leave me alone!"

His smile slipped. "You are a cambion—it is in your nature to seek power. That is why you will not reject the amulet I have given you." He leaned closer, resting his hand on his cane. "The deadline to enroll at the Scholomance is midnight on the winter solstice. Don't be late."

The invisible forces around my arm and ankles vanished, and I stumbled back a step. Dazed, I looked around. The other students had gone, and the last school bus was driving away down the street. I still clutched the necklace and the parchment, but Asmodeus was nowhere to be seen. I frowned at the objects in my hand and raised my fist, about to fling them to the ground and stomp on them, but I felt something strange.

My heart missed a beat. I tugged out the necklace, letting the red jewel dangle in the air. I wasn't sure, but I thought I could feel something from the scarlet jewel. It was a little different from before—more resolute than calm—but still, it reminded me of what I had felt in the woods and in my mother's workshop.

With trembling hands, I unzipped my satchel and stuffed the scroll and the necklace inside. When I got home, I would show them to my mom, and I would tell her what Asmodeus had said to me. At least, that's what I told myself I would do.

* * *

My mom was at the kitchen table, sipping a cup of tea. "Lesley, you're late. Is something wrong?"

"I missed the bus," I muttered.

"Oh, sweetie." She hugged me.

Once she released me from her hug, I reached for the zipper of my satchel. From within came the rustle of parchment and the tinkle of gold chain. "Mom," I began.

"Yes, Lesley?"

I hesitated. "I was wondering... since you're a witch and my father was an incubus, doesn't that mean I should have magical abilities too?"

For the briefest moment, fear flashed across my mother's face. She smoothed the expression away quickly, but it was enough to reveal the truth. *Oh my god.*

She smiled sadly. "I'm sorry, but there's no guarantee you would have inherited abilities from either me or your father."

I felt a knot in my stomach but hid my reaction as best I could. "Oh, okay. I was just wondering. Because, you know, it would be, like, *so* cool if I had powers like yours."

"Trust me, sweetie, magic is way more trouble than it's worth."

She's afraid I'll find out... she doesn't want me to know. I lowered my hand from the zipper of the satchel. "Yeah, you're probably right." I turned away, trudging down the hall to my bedroom and trying to keep the wetness in my eyes from spilling over. I glanced back over my shoulder at my mother. *Why would you lie to me?*

* * *

That night, I couldn't sleep. I squinted at the clock radio on my nightstand. It was after midnight. The only light in my room was the faint glow of a street lamp seeping between the slats of my window blinds. My guitar stood propped up in the corner, its strings gleaming eerily in the dim light.

The books atop my dresser looked like teeth jutting from a giant's lower jaw. My jacket, draped over the desk chair, could have been a huge sleeping bat.

My gaze slid to the jewelry box atop my dresser, and my heart thumped. "No..." I tried to tell myself. But it was driving me crazy—I had to know for sure. I slid out of bed and opened the jewelry box. Inside, the amulet's jewel glowed, its crimson light pulsing in time with my heartbeat. I took out the crinkled scroll and unrolled it. I was able to read it under the glow of the necklace. On the scroll, written in angular letters, were five spells. The first was titled *To Create Light* and listed a single magic word. The second and third, labeled *To Create Force* and *To Create Fire*, were also single words. The fourth, which was three words long, was titled *To Open Locks*. The fifth and final spell was longer still. It was accompanied by a diagram of a circle filled with runes and angular shapes. The instructions said to trace the circle on the ground and set up candles around it before speaking the incantation. It was labeled *To Summon a Servant of Asmodeus*.

I set down the scroll and, with trembling hands, picked up the necklace and clasped it around my neck. The scarlet jewel felt warm against my skin. At the same moment, a sense of resolve washed over me. For a while, I stood there, basking in the calm the amulet gave me. I took up the scroll again and peered at the first spell. "*Lux*," I whispered.

A pinprick of scarlet light appeared in the air, shimmering for a moment before fading away. My mouth hung open in disbelief. *It worked.* My heart was racing. *It actually worked! I can do magic!*

I looked at my hand. "*Lux!*" This time, I spoke the word with more confidence. A tiny orb of light flickered into existence, hovering in the air above my palm—just where I had imagined it would. It filled my room with a dim, red glow, and this time it didn't go out. My pulse raced. I moved my hand and smiled when the light moved along with it, as if I were holding the luminous orb.

I held the light close to the scroll, reading the next spell. I turned my gaze toward the row of books atop my dresser. "*Impulsio.*" The books fell over like dominoes. I opened my hand, releasing the glowing orb, and the light winked out. I spoke the next spell, "*Ignis.*" I smiled with delight as a crimson candle flame leaped to life, hovering above my palm.

My smiled faded. "No!" I whispered in horror. I released my grip, and the scarlet fire went out. I tore off the necklace, stuffed it and the scroll into the jewelry box, and slammed the lid shut. "No... this is what he wants. This is exactly what Asmodeus wants me to do." I threw myself back down on my bed and pulled up the covers, shivering as I cocooned myself in my wings.

6

The Library

As the weeks went on, I tried to forget about the calm I felt from being in the woods and from wearing the amulet Asmodeus had given me. I tried to convince myself my mom was right—magic was too much trouble to deal with. My life had become weird enough already. No need to make it even weirder, right? But it still hurt that she hadn't been honest with me.

The gears of my bicycle whirred as I peddled along the sidewalk. The afternoon sun shone through wispy clouds, and the breeze streaming past me was pleasantly cool. I held my wings spread, my tail out behind me for balance. I wondered if this was what flying would be like.

I approached a low, broad building behind a row of neatly trimmed bushes. I veered my bike into the parking lot and waited in front of the building. A couple of minutes later, a car pulled into the lot. It was a black Mustang with dark tinted windows and a pair of red racing stripes painted along its length. The driver's door opened just a crack, and a black parasol popped open out of it. Sadie emerged, holding the opaque umbrella above her head. A moment later, Zack got out from the passenger side. "Thanks for the ride," he said.

We headed inside the library. Rows of bookshelves stood along the sides of the spacious room. Tables and chairs were clustered in an open area beyond the *New Releases* stand, and the circulation desk stood at the back. A man with a long white beard—and huge gossamer dragonfly wings sprouting from his back—stood behind the desk.

Sadie folded up her parasol. "So you've never been here before?" she asked me.

"Nope," I replied.

"Then I think you're in for a treat."

"What do you mean by that?"

Sadie smirked. "You'll see."

We headed to one of the tables in the middle of the room. Near the end of a row of books, a bespectacled woman hovered in the air. Butterfly wings fluttered between her shoulders as she arranged some books along a top shelf. "Are all the librarians here fairies?" I asked.

"Not all, but a lot of them are," Sadie replied. "You have to have magical abilities to be able to work here."

"Why is that?"

"Like I said, you'll see." She sat in one of the chairs. "I need to get started on my homework. Zack, wanna give Lesley a tour?"

"Uh, sure." Zack pointed to the bookshelves along one side. "Here, come on."

I followed as he stepped into an aisle between the bookshelves. My heart thumped a little faster at the thought of being alone with him, but a knot formed in my stomach. Zack had been nice to me, but was he just being polite? Did he find my demonic features unsettling? Was he just putting up with me right now?

Because of my anxious thoughts, I hardly noticed something strange was happening to the bookshelves. When I finally did, I nearly stumbled. The aisle was much longer than before, *way* too long to fit inside the library. I squinted into the distance. "What the…"

Zack smiled. "It's magic."

"Magic?"

"We call it the Labyrinth. The way Sadie explained it is that books aren't that different from magic spells. When enough books are gathered together, it creates a place hidden between other places, similar to the Sacred Grove. The effect is strongest near a wellspring, so the librarians here have to use magic to keep it under control—especially to keep things from escaping."

"Things… escaping?"

"Yeah."

"Like… escaping from the books?"

"Yep."

"That's crazy!"

A harsh "shhh!" came from the butterfly-winged librarian, who raised a finger to her lips, looking sternly at me. She stood at the end of the aisle—which had returned to normal. The aisle stretched from the central area to the wall and no further.

The librarian strode away around the corner. I followed Zack again. With each step, the aisle stretched longer and longer, until it seemed to reach to infinity. Side passages that hadn't been there before began to branch off.

Zack grinned at me. "Come on, let's keep exploring."

I followed as he turned at a junction. We entered an aisle wider than the others. Couches and potted plants lined the aisle below bookshelves that rose two stories high. Rolling ladders in tracks rose toward a skylight above.

We turned down another side passage, one with children's books on the shelves and toys scattered all over the floor. As we went further, the toys grew larger, until I stepped under an archway of alphabet blocks and past dolls and teddy bears as big as I was.

"Oh, let's go this way!" I turned down another aisle that looked like a science museum. Taxidermied animals and mounted skeletons stood in glass cases along the aisle. The shelves were lined entirely with biology textbooks. A moment later, a voice came from another side passage. I peered in. Something about the aisle beyond seemed familiar.

"Did you hear that?" I asked Zack.

He shook his head.

I stepped through the passage, cocking my head to listen. This aisle was narrower than the others, and the floor was no longer carpeted but covered in linoleum tiles. The voice came again, and I remembered why the aisle seemed so familiar. I turned the other way, almost hitting Zack as I did. But the museum-like passage wasn't there anymore. Only a wall of bookshelves stood in front of me.

"Zack," I said, "how did we get here?"

He glanced around. "Where is here?"

"It's the library at my old school! From before I—"

His eyes widened. "You mean there are humans here?"

"Lesley?" The voice came from the next aisle over. A knot formed in my stomach. Phyllis! It had been her voice I'd heard. Her footsteps drew closer. "Lesley, is that you?"

"Zack," I whispered. "I can't let her see me like this! How do we go back?"

"You need to be calm. It only works if you mind is clear. Close your eyes, and think of the Misty Hollow library."

I tried, but my heart was pounding as the sound of Phyllis's footsteps drew closer. "It's not working!" I gave him a pleading look. "Can't *you* get us out of here?"

"I can only get myself out of here. I can't bring you with me." Zack took a breath. "Think of how the bookshelves looked," he said, his voice calm and steady. "Think of how quiet it was, of the smell of the paper." He placed his hands on my shoulders. I wrapped my arms around him, drawing him close.

I realized I didn't hear Phyllis's footsteps anymore. Slowly, I opened my eyes and was once more among the bookshelves of the library in Misty Hollow. Then I realized I was hugging Zack. My cheeks went warm, and I pulled my arms away from him.

He stepped back from me, glancing away. "Uh, yeah, I forgot to mention how the Labyrinth connects to other libraries." He cleared his throat. "Who was that, anyway?"

"That was Phyllis." I gestured at myself. "Before *this* happened to me, she was my best friend." I looked at Zack. "Wait, did you say *other* libraries? What other libraries?"

"All libraries, as far as I know."

My eyes widened, my sadness forgotten. "This place is amazing!"

From the next aisle over, the librarian gave another harsh "shh!"

"Sorry," I whispered.

* * *

In my room that evening, I stared at a blank paper that was supposed to be my math homework. I couldn't concentrate. I chewed my lip, my gaze drawn to the jewelry box atop my dresser. I got up and reached to open the box.

No, I told myself. I turned away, picked up my phone from the desk. I opened a message meant for Phyllis. Since what had happened at the library that day, she'd been on my mind. *Things have been crazy lately,* I typed. *Sorry I haven't contacted you sooner. Do you have time to talk now?* I hesitated a while before hitting the send button.

Less than a minute later, my phone buzzed. I answered. "Oh my god, Lesley!" came Phyllis's voice. "I was worried sick! Where have you been?"

I remembered what Sadie had said about the fae not wanting to draw attention to themselves. Would I get in trouble for telling Phyllis the truth? Then I saw my dim reflection in my bedroom window, the horns poking out from my forehead, and I shuddered. I didn't ever want her to see me this way. "I'm *so* sorry. Mom and I had to leave town suddenly."

"It's been nearly a month. You haven't called or texted or anything. What happened?"

I went through the story I'd been working on in my mind. "Um, so... my dad... he found us. He's a really bad guy. I was afraid to call at first because... because I thought he might trace my phone or something."

"Oh my god. Your dad is, like, abusive?"

"Yeah... something like that."

"Are you safe? Do you need help?"

"It's fine. Mom and I are safe now." That was probably a lie, though.

"Will I ever see you again?"

"I-I don't know."

A long pause. "I'm just glad you're still okay. We can still call each other, right?"

"Of course we can."

"It's the funniest thing… I was just thinking about you. In the school library today, I *swear* I heard you talking to someone. And now you finally called me."

I chewed my lip. "That's so weird." I tried to sound normal. "So, school is going all right?"

"Same as usual. What about you? I guess you're going to a different school now."

"Yeah. It's been *so* stressful getting used to all the… getting used to everything."

"I bet. Any cute boys there?"

I blushed. "Well, um, there is this one boy named Zack."

"Ooh! What's he like?"

"I don't know if I should—"

"Come on, it's not like I'll be able to blab any of this to him."

I smiled. "Okay then. Zack… he has the most handsome silver eyes. He's new in town too, actually…"

We chatted for a long while, and by the time we said goodbye, I was feeling much better. I set down the phone and leaned back in my chair, letting out a contented sigh. But it wasn't long before a feeling of longing crept through me again. I missed Phyllis. I missed my old school and the town I'd grown up in. I looked again at the jewelry box on top of my dresser. I could be human again. All I had to do was…

"No," I said to myself. I pulled my gaze away from the box and tried once again to concentrate on my homework.

* * *

The weather grew colder, the last warmth of summer fading into the chill of autumn. I kept up with school as best I could, but deep inside, anxiety gnawed at me. The thought of Asmodeus's offer—the thought of becoming human again—wouldn't leave me alone.

"Lesley, are you okay?" Jeremy asked as we waited for history class to begin. He sat in the desk next to mine. "You looked like you were zoning out."

"I guess I kind of was."

"Anything on your mind?"

I hesitated. "No, I-I'm fine."

The school bell rang. Mrs. Osborn stepped into the classroom. Instead of her usual smug expression, the wiry-haired elf's brow was crinkled in surprise. "Good morning, class." She held up a roll of paper—smooth white paper stamped with a seal of gray wax. "It seems that the Morrigan has issued a decree."

I blinked. "The Morrigan?" I felt like I should recognize that name.

Nerissa, seated in the row ahead of me, glanced back. "Yeah, Lesley. You know... the queen of the fae?"

"Oh, right. Now I remember." In some of her stories, my mom had mentioned that the fae were ruled by a queen known as the Morrigan.

"Ahem." Mrs. Osborn shot a glance at Nerissa and me. "The Morrigan has decreed that, as part of the coming Samhain festival, teachers shall"—she peered at the scroll through her half-moon glasses—"shall have their students take part in an activity that fosters a renewed understanding between the Seelie and Unseelie." She rolled her eyes.

"I can't believe you forgot we had a queen," Nerissa whispered to me.

"Shut up, Riss," I hissed back.

"To comply with this decree," Mrs. Osborn continued, "I've decided you will do group reports on the history of a fae tribe of your choosing. Each team will consist of one Seelie and one Unseelie member." She narrowed her eyes in my direction. "Lesley, Nerissa, since you two seem to be on such friendly terms, why don't you set an example and become our first team?"

I blinked. Nerissa stared back at me in disbelief.

The other students were already rising from their desks. I looked around as my classmates shuffled around the room, but everyone avoided eye contact with me. I turned to Jeremy, giving him a desperate look. He shrugged, pointing to the centaur boy he'd taking a seat next to. "Sorry. I, uh, I can't be with another Unseelie, remember?"

The shuffling settled down as quickly as it had started. Panicking, I glanced around again. Everyone was already paired up—nobody wanted to team up with either of us. I looked back at Nerissa. She scanned the room helplessly before turning to me again.

"Great," I muttered to her. "Just great. I guess we're a team."

"I'm not any more happy about this than you are, Lesley."

"This is all your fault."

"Shut up, freak."

The Altar

The students bustled through the school's front doors, out into a cold, cloudy afternoon. Instead of following them to the buses along the street, I turned toward the student parking lot. Among the parked cars, Nerissa sat in a silver convertible.

"Nice car," I said as I approached.

She frowned at me. "I still can't believe I'm stuck with you for this project."

I struck a pose, unfurling my wings and curling my tail to the side. "What? Are you embarrassed to be seen with a lowly Unseelie?"

She rolled her eyes. "Just get in the car."

Nerissa drove us to the nicer part of town up in the hills overlooking the valley. The streets wound over the gently rolling slopes, past houses that stood two or even three stories tall. She parked the car in front of a cream-colored house perched on a hillside. I picked up my satchel and followed her in.

A chandelier hung from the ceiling of the foyer. Ahead, an archway opened to a spacious kitchen, and to one side, a staircase curved up to an indoor balcony. Pictures lined the walls, and in the corner stood a grandfather clock. Other than the ticking of the clock, the house was silent.

I glanced at the portraits hanging on the walls. Among them, a picture showed a distinguished looking elf couple and a sweetly smiling Nerissa. Again, I noticed how silent the house was.

"Aren't your parents home?" I asked.

"Ha! No," Nerissa called from the kitchen.

"What do you mean by that?"

"They're hardly ever home." She leaned against one side of the archway. "Dad is always away on 'important business.'"

I peeked into an adjacent sitting room, where more pictures decorated the walls. In one, a male elf was posing heroically with a bow and arrow in hand. Another showed a pair of young elf women dancing, their dresses twirling as flower petals drifted around them. A large picture in the center showed the same elf couple surrounded by four others, including a younger looking Nerissa. "These are pictures of your family?"

"No, they're pictures of complete strangers." Nerissa rolled her eyes. "Yes, Lesley, they're obviously my family."

I noticed a picture of Nerissa in a sparkling ballet dress, pirouetting with her arms in the air. "You do ballet?"

She shrugged. "It was my parents' idea."

I scrunched my brow. "You don't *like* ballet?"

"Doesn't really matter, does it?" She headed back into the kitchen.

I peered through the archway, watching as Nerissa pulled a book from her backpack. As she did, something else rolled out—a crudely carved wooden rod that looked suspiciously like a magic wand. Her back was turned, so she didn't see me watching as she quickly put the wand away again. When I stepped into the kitchen, I pretended I hadn't seen.

I sat at the table across from her and unzipped my satchel, pulling out a book of my own. Nerissa ignored me as she flipped through the pages of hers. "Your parents make you do ballet," I asked, "even though you don't like it?"

Nerissa looked up, shooting a glare at me. "Why do you care? Let's just focus on this stupid project, okay?"

"Okay," I muttered.

* * *

Cold raindrops pattered on the sidewalk. My bike's tires splashed through puddles as I pedaled past storefront windows. My jacket was zipped up tight. I wished I'd worn my winter coat instead, but I couldn't until I figured out how to cut slits for my wings without ruining the stuffing. Needless to say, I wasn't in the best of moods, and not just because of the weather.

Even though we'd worked together only once so far, I was already sure Nerissa was the worst group partner possible. Yesterday at her house, she second-guessed everything I did. We were supposed to meet up again that evening, and I was dreading it. I'd messaged Sadie, and she'd invited me over to blow off steam. She'd also claimed to know how I should deal with Nerissa, and I was eager—almost desperate—to hear Sadie's advice.

Among the storefronts along the street was a flower shop. Beneath the awning, colorful bouquets were on display outside the entrance. A warm, inviting glow came from the windows, pushing back the gray of the dreary afternoon. I rolled my bike to a stop beneath the awning. Inside the shop were stands arranged with flowers of all kinds. By the counter at the back, dressed in a store uniform and busy tending one of the stands, what my mother.

I stepped up to her. "Hey, Mom."

"Hi, sweetie." She tilted her head at me. "Is something the matter?"

"Just my group project with Nerissa. I can't stand her!" I sighed. "Anyway, Sadie invited me over to her house and I'm headed there now, but since I was coming past here I thought I'd stop in." I glanced around the store. "So, you liking the new job?"

"Oh, yes," my mother replied. "My gardening skills are coming in handy after all."

"Don't sell yourself short, Jane." A man with antlers sprouting from his forehead peered out through the door to the back room. "You have a green thumb. I'm surprised you didn't decide to become a dryad." He glanced at me. "This is your daughter?"

The antlered man turned to me. His smile slipped as his gaze darted to the spots above my shoulders, where my wing-claws hovered, then to my forehead, where my devil horns protruded. "Uh, it's a pleasure to meet you," he mumbled, ducking into the back room again.

Once more, I sighed. My mom cast a sidelong glance at the doorway. She took my hands, squeezing them encouragingly. "Don't mind him, sweetie."

"I know, I know. He's probably never seen a cambion before, just like everyone else in town."

After chatting with my mom a bit, I headed back out into the rain and pedaled my bike down one of the side streets. The trees along the winding lane seemed ancient—huge, gnarled things that stretched their branches out over the street so it was almost like a tunnel. Houses and cottages lay hidden in the shadows beneath them.

I came to a length of wrought-iron fence along one side of the street. Beyond it stood an old Victorian-style house. Hedges loomed on all sides of the yard, and trees reached out their branches. If the sun had been out, the entire yard would probably have still been in shadow.

I skidded to a stop in front of the gate. I swallowed and pressed the button on the intercom panel. "Hello?" No one replied. "Hello? This is Lesley."

After a few seconds, the gate swung inward. I hesitated and pedaled my bike through. A flagstone path led from the driveway to the front porch. I rolled to a stop, peering up at the old mansion. In every way, it looked like a haunted house. I set my bike down on the lawn and crept up the front steps. Hesitantly, I knocked on the door. "Hello? Sadie?" The door opened with an ominous creak. Inside, it was dark. I bit my lip and stepped through.

My eyes took a few seconds to adjust to the dimness. I almost jumped when I noticed a tall, gaunt figure standing by the door, holding it open for me. Long, claw-like nails grew from his gnarled hands. His skin was white as chalk, and his head was completely bald. He wore a black suit and tie like a corpse dressed up for a funeral. His glassy eyes stared at nothing in particular, and he stood unnaturally still.

I gulped. "Uh... hi? Is Sadie here?"

The man's head swiveled toward me. His lips parted in what was probably meant to be a smile. Inside his mouth, fangs glistened.

Footsteps came from the staircase. I turned and saw Sadie gliding down the stairs. "Lesley," she purred, "so good of you to come over."

The swishing of my tail grew faster. I looked at the other vampire. "Sadie, this is... your father?"

"No, this is Rupert. He's our butler." Sadie stepped over to the unmoving figure and gave him a hug. Rupert didn't seem to notice. "The poor thing doesn't have a soul," Sadie explained. "But don't worry, my father has him good and mesmerized. Otherwise Rupert here would be getting himself into all sorts of trouble."

I peered warily at the gaunt figure. He gave me another rictus smile. "Mesmerized?" I murmured.

"Yep. Most vampires have hypnotic abilities. Of course, we don't just use them to turn lesser undead into our minions. It's also quite useful for luring in victims."

I swallowed. "Victims?"

The room was getting dimmer. I glanced back to see Rupert closing the door. The glassy-eyed vampire latched it shut and stepped in front of it like a guard taking his post.

"The easy way is to just sneak into someone's bedroom at night," Sadie said. "But I think it's *so* much more fun to win a victim's trust first, then watch as she walks right into my trap." Her fangs glistened unnervingly as she smiled. "Now then, I think I'll have something to drink."

I stepped away from her, glancing this way and that in search of an escape route—but Sadie burst out laughing.

"I'm kidding, Lesley! I'm just kidding." She pointed at me. "Oh my god, you should see the look on your face!"

"Very funny, Sadie." I curled one hand into a fist and pretended to punch her shoulder. "Actually," I said with a laugh, "that *was* a pretty good prank. You had me going there for a second."

"I'm not very good at mesmerizing," Sadie continued, "and besides, I would never use it on one of my classmates. As for the drink, I was actually thinking of trying some tea. Would you like some too?"

"Uh, sure."

"Ah, but what you don't realize is that my kind invitation is merely another deception... just kidding, just kidding!" Sadie laughed, dodging another fake punch.

She led me through the parlor and into the kitchen. A pair of windows looked out over the back yard, but the view was mostly blocked by the thorny vines of some rose bushes. An archway opened to the dining room, which held a table long enough to seat a dozen people.

Sadie rummaged through the cabinets. "We only keep the stuff around in case we have guests over—which isn't very often, come to think of it." She found a couple of porcelain cups, some saucers, and a jar filled with dried tea leaves. Digging around some more, she pulled out a tarnished kettle. She set it on the counter and turned to me. "So, um, I've actually never had tea before and have no idea how to make it."

I gave her a smile. "Don't worry, my mom makes tea for me all the time." I took the kettle over to the sink and filled it with water.

Before long, we were sitting in the dining room, each sipping a cup of tea. "How do you like it?" I asked.

She looked at me and at the steaming teacup in her hand. "Um, it's all right." After a moment of hesitation, she took another tiny sip.

"You think it's awful, don't you?"

She frowned. "It's so thin and watery. Obviously, I'm more used to—" She seemed to notice my discomfort and changed the subject. "So, how's your group project coming?"

"Ugh... Nerissa is a *such* a pain. I have to go to her house again in like an hour, but I *so* don't want to. You said you know how I should deal with her?"

Sadie leaned forward, resting her elbows on the table. "Okay, this may sound crazy, but just hear me out. You could try being nice to her."

"Wait... *that's* your advice?" I sighed. "And here I was hoping you knew some dark secret that I could blackmail her with."

"Well, in my experience, being nice to people can work wonders." She crooked an eyebrow at me.

"You're right," I admitted. "If not for you, I'd probably be sitting by myself at lunch." I took a deep breath. "I'll consider your advice. I'll try to be—ugh—*nice* to her."

* * *

The rain had let up by the time I got back from Nerissa's house. She'd been infuriating as expected, and I'd quickly given up on the idea that being nice might change that. I was still frustrated when I'd gotten home, so I'd decided to go for a walk through the neighborhood.

Beyond the rooftops, the setting sun was shining through ragged gaps in the clouds, turning the sky orange and gold. By now, the leaves were changing color, so the trees were painted with the same hues as the sunset sky.

I heard a rustle, then footsteps across the pavement. I glanced back in time to see a girl about my age hurry across the street and disappear into the bushes. The hood of her jacket was up, so I couldn't see her face, but I did glimpse a few strands of blond hair. "Nerissa?" I murmured.

I strode over to the spot where she had vanished. A drainage ditch ran perpendicular to the street, flowing into a culvert that ran beneath the road. Bushes and trees grew along the embankment, filling the ditch with shadows. The sound of trickling water echoed from the dimness below. I listened for a moment and heard faint footsteps crunching across the gravel.

"Nerissa?" I called out. "If you're planning to jump out and scare me, it won't work." My tail swished as I crept down the embankment and into the ditch.

Dust drifted in the rays of fading sunlight. The air was filled with the scent of mud and rotting vegetation. Water flowed along the ditch's pebbly bottom, into the concrete archway of the culvert. "Riss, or whoever you are, come out!" I noticed something lying within the darkness inside the culvert. I took out my phone, holding it up as a flashlight. I crept forward, ducking my head as I stepped inside the concrete tunnel that ran under the street.

Resting against the wall, a stack of wooden boards had been piled into a low, makeshift table. Half-melted candles surrounded a pair of items—an animal skull that might have belonged to a raccoon and an old leather-bound book. On the wall behind the table, strange symbols were drawn in white chalk. Traced on the pebbly ground in front of the altar, half washed away by the flowing water, was a large circle filled with runes and angular shapes. I gasped—it looked like the diagram of the summoning circle from the scroll Asmodeus had given me. I reached out and flipped open the book. Scrawled on one of the pages was a drawing of a horned, winged beast.

Footsteps approached me from behind. I bit my lip, stifling a scream as I hurried away from the sound. As fast as I could, I scrambled up out of the ditch and dashed away along the sidewalk.

* * *

After school the next day, I stood at the bottom of the ditch at the entrance to the culvert. The afternoon sun shone through the trees, casting dappled light along the earthen embankment. Compared to yesterday, the flow of water had slowed to a shallow trickle. I peered into the dimness within the concrete archway, but nothing was inside the tunnel except gravel and mud.

Sadie clutched her parasol in her hand, holding it up against the dappled sunlight. In addition to carrying the opaque umbrella, she wore dark sunglasses and a wide-brimmed hat. With an uneasy expression, she watched the trickle of water that ran across the pebbles at her feet.

I looked at her. "Is something wrong, Sadie?"

"The undead fear running water," she murmured.

Further up the ditch, Jeremy was sniffing around. "I can't tell for sure," he said to me. "There might be a scent trail here, but I think the creek washed most of it away." He stepped toward the concrete archway. "Where did you say this girl was?"

I pointed at the embankment. "She came right down there, past where the altar was. I thought it might have been Nerissa, but I wasn't sure."

"Maybe I could tell if I was in my other form." Jeremy kicked off his shoes. He reached down to lift his shirt but hesitated. "Uh, could you give me a bit of privacy?"

"Oh, right." Sadie and I turned away, and I covered my eyes.

Jeremy grunted, and I winced at what sounded like his bones creaking. His pained grunts grew lower, becoming animal growls. Once the growling stopped, I turned to find Jeremy kneeling there, breathing heavily. He was half again as tall as before, his now muscular upper body covered in shaggy fur. Claws grew from his fingertips, and his face had elongated into a wolf-like snout. After a moment, he rose onto feet that were now paws and stuffed his shirt, socks, and sneakers into his backpack.

"Does it hurt to change form?" I asked.

He gave me a shrug before kneeling down to sniff at the ground. He grunted, pointing up at the embankment.

"You found a scent trail?"

He nodded. Sadie and I followed him up out of the ditch. Jeremy stooped low, sniffing as the three of us headed along the sidewalk. He stepped into a clump of trees, and we continued uphill. Before long, we emerged into the ritzy neighborhood. Jeremy came to a stop in front of a cream-colored house on a hillside.

Sadie peered through her sunglasses. "Is that..."

"Yeah. That's Nerissa's house." I turned to Sadie. "What am I supposed to do? She's coming over to my house later for our group project!"

"If Nerissa really is up to no good," Sadie said, "I'd say that's all the more reason to be nice to her."

8

Secrets

Nerissa stepped into the foyer. She raised an eyebrow as she peered into the front room. "How quaint."

I bit my lip, holding in a retort. "We can go to my room if you want. It's probably more comfortable than the kitchen."

I led her down the hall. The afternoon sunlight streamed in through my bedroom window, falling across my desk. I pulled out the desk chair and turned it toward the bed, offering Nerissa a seat, but she ignored it. She was too busy looking around my room. Her gaze fell on a leather-bound booklet atop my dresser.

"Ooh, what's this?" Nerissa tugged at the clasp that held the cover shut.

"That's just my diary," I said, gently taking the booklet from her and setting it down on my nightstand.

She reached for the jewelry box. "And what's in here?"

I snatched the box from her. "Don't open that!"

She blinked at me. "Okay, jeez."

I gestured to my desk chair, and finally she sat down. She opened her backpack and took out a couple of books along with her notes for the project. I chewed my lip.

She frowned at me. "Oh, what is it now?"

I decided to try Sadie's advice again. "I, um, I'm sorry we didn't get along so well before," I lied. "I'm willing to put that behind us if you are."

Nerissa rolled her eyes. "Wow, Lesley. I never figured you were the goodie-two-shoes type."

I couldn't keep the anger out of my voice. "Why? Because I'm half demon, therefore I must be evil?"

She blinked. "Well, uh…"

"Never mind." I sat down on the bed. "Um, I did want to ask you something. Your parents *make* you do ballet? You must be under a lot of pressure to live up to their expectations."

"Oh, you think you have me all figured out?"

"No, I…" I sighed again. "I'm just trying to understand your situation."

For once, Nerissa actually didn't seem annoyed. "You're right, though," she admitted. "It seems like my parents are always on my case about something. I wish I could have it as easy as you do."

I tried hard not to sound angry again. "What do you mean by that?"

"Uh, like, nobody expects someone like *you* to be perfect."

"Wait… *that's* how you see things?"

"You're not the one with the impossible standard to live up to. Nobody expects *you* to always be prim and proper and graceful *all the time*. Nobody cares if you slip up even once."

Even though I was a bit frustrated, I couldn't help but feel sorry for her. "Riss, I didn't realize things were like that for you. But I don't think you understand what things are like for me."

"Oh? And how are things for you, Lesley?"

"It's no cakewalk for me either. I was hoping people would have stopped whispering behind my back by now, but..." I shook my head. "The other day, I heard a rumor that I sometimes sneak into people's bedrooms at night and suck their breath like how a vampire sucks blood, paralyzing my victims and causing nightmares."

Nerissa tilted her head. "Well... do you?"

"No!" I rolled my eyes at her. "That's not even a thing cambions do."

"Good to know. Um, what other rumors have you heard?"

I paused, wondering how much I should tell her. Well, I *was* trying to be nice to her. "I overheard some people say they're afraid of me. Like they thought I might tie them up and torture them or something. But the worst one was that since technically I'm half succubus—which, by the way, is a *sex demon*—some people think I must be a total slut."

Nerissa looked at me. "Wow, it sounds like life sucks for you just as much as it does for me." She offered a hand. "Sorry I was mean."

I blinked in surprise. *She's actually apologizing?* A moment later, I shook her hand. "It's okay. Um, so, promise you won't tell anyone else those things I just told you?"

She smiled. "Cross my heart."

* * *

At school the next day, people seemed to be looking at me funny—more so than usual, I mean.

I shuffled along the crowded hallway, glancing out of the corners of my eyes. As I passed by my classmates, some would fall silent then whisper to one another once I'd gone past. Others would avoid eye contact with me. My brow furrowed more deeply as I continued along the hall.

The kitsune girl and her harpy friend went wide-eyed as I approached. I wrinkled my nose. "What are you looking at?"

"We're sorry, we're sorry!" the fox-girl yelped. "Please don't hurt us!"

I blinked. "Hurt you? I wouldn't—"

Another girl stepped up to me. "You!" she said, pointing an accusing finger. Witch-fire flared in her eyes. "It's *your* fault, isn't it?"

"What?" I asked.

"I've been having *nightmares* all week," she snapped. "Whatever you're doing to me, stop it!"

"Nightmares? Wait a second, where did you hear that I—" But she had already stomped away into the crowd.

A knot formed in my stomach. I hurried along, but from behind came a sneering voice along with the sound of clicking hooves. "Hey, Lesley."

I groaned. "Not now, Murk." I picked up my pace, but his hooves clicked faster, keeping up with me as the satyr-boy repeated my name. Finally, I spun to face him. "Ugh, what is it?"

"You're half succubus, right?" Murk struck a swaggering pose. "Why don't you go ahead and *suck* my—"

"Augh! Murk!" I turned away in disgust. "Wait, where did you hear that?" I asked, facing him again.

He frowned. "Hear what?"

"That I'm"—I lowered my voice—"that I'm half succubus."

Murk shrugged. "I heard Pauline and Daphne talking about it."

"Nerissa's friends?" I clenched my teeth as I marched along the hallway, shoving my way through the doors to the cafeteria. "Nerissa!" The chattering of my classmates quieted as I stormed into the room, my tail whipping side to side.

I saw them—the gossamer-winged fairy, the copper-haired centaur, and the blond elf. My wings flared as I strode up to their table. Nerissa's eyes widened as she saw me. "Lesley? What's the matter?"

"You *told* them!" I hissed. "You told them, didn't you?"

Nerissa turned to Daphne and Pauline. Daphne's wings fluttered nervously, and Pauline's horse tail swished. Both girls avoided eye contact with me. "Oh my god," Nerissa muttered. She turned to me again. "Lesley—"

"You blabbed that stuff to them, and now the whole school is talking about it! You said you'd keep those things secret. You promised!"

"Yeah? Well, there's nothing I can do about it now, is there? So go sit down and leave us alone."

I ground my teeth. "You know what, Riss?" I unzipped my satchel and pulled out a notebook, slapping it down on the table in front of her. "Forget our group project! I'll do a different one on my own."

Nerissa glared at me. "Fine," she said.

"Fine!" I yelled back. I turned, stalking away from the table.

From behind my back, I heard her murmur "freak."

I stopped and slowly turned. "What did you just call me?"

Nerissa rose from her seat. "You heard me. I said you're a *freak*!" She strode up, facing me nose to nose.

Some of the students around us gasped. Pauline's hooves clacked as she followed Nerissa around the table. "Hey! Break it up!"

I sneered at Nerissa. "I thought elves were supposed to be all prim and proper and graceful. I don't know how everybody keeps mistaking *you* for one."

She scowled. "Did you just insult me?"

"Yes, I obviously did, but I guess you're too *stupid* to understand even that."

Her jaw dropped. "What? How dare you!"

"And do you know what else? You're never going to live up to your parent's expectations. Do you realize that? Nothing you do will ever be good enough for them!"

Her voice quavered. "You take that back!"

"First take back what you said! Take back that I'm a freak!"

With a grunt, Nerissa shoved me. I staggered back, my wings fluttering for balance. Once I found my footing, I clenched my fists.

Feeling a hand on my shoulder, I glanced back at Sadie. "Lesley, stop!" she warned. "Stop before you get in trouble."

But I didn't listen. The scaly edge of my wing rasped against Sadie's wrist as I pulled away from her grip. I dove forward, plowing into Nerissa and knocking her to the floor. I dropped to my knees, crouching over her as I grabbed a bundle of her shirt sleeve. I raised my other fist in the air, aiming it right at Nerissa's stupid face.

I hesitated. Around me, the cafeteria had gone silent. Nerissa had thrown her hands up in front of her, peering up at me with a look of fright. I sucked in a ragged breath through my teeth. Slowly, I lowered my trembling fist and released my grip on her sleeve. Pauline took Nerissa's hand, helping her to her feet. Moisture glistened in Nerissa's eyes as she glowered at me.

I suddenly realized that everyone was watching me. Hiding my face in my hands, I dashed out of the cafeteria.

* * *

The ticking of the clock filled the silent, empty hallway. I slumped in one of the chairs outside the principal's office, my wings draped around my shoulders.

The office door opened, and Nerissa stepped out. She sniffed, wiping at her face, and grimaced at me. "Your turn, freak." She marched past me, heading away down the hall.

My tail twitched. I rose and stepped into the office. Principal Constance narrowed her eyes at me. She pointed to one of the chairs. Without a word, I sat down. "What do you have to say for yourself, Miss Robinson?" the principal asked.

I kept my gaze on the floor. "I'm not just going to blame Nerissa. It was my fault too. I'm really, *really* sorry for what happened."

"When we first met, you admitted you have sharp claws and that your horns and tail barb are sharp as well. During the scuffle, did you have any intention of using them?"

I looked up at her. "No, of course not."

"Oh, come now, Miss Robinson, it must have at least crossed your mind that you could slash Nerissa with your claws or stab her with your horns."

"Well, yeah, it did *occur* to me, but I would never—"

Principal Constance wrote in her notes, murmuring aloud as she did. "Has violent thoughts about attacking others with horns and claws."

"Hey, I didn't say that!" I rose from my chair. "Listen to me! All I meant was…"

"Tries to intimidate others with displays of her demonic features," the principal continued.

I glanced back to find my tail whipping from side to side, my wings flared. I quickly stilled and folded them. The principal glared at me, as if daring me to keep talking. Slowly, I returned to my seat.

"Do you have anything else to say, Miss Robinson?"

I kept my mouth shut.

"Very well. I'll let you off with a warning for now, but if you slip up again, you *will* be disciplined." She looked me in the eye. "I will be watching you closely from now on, Miss Robinson. Do *not* cross me again. Understood?"

I swallowed and nodded.

She pointed to the door. "You are dismissed."

* * *

My mother was waiting for me when I got home. She stood in the foyer, her hands on her hips. Wordlessly, she pointed to the couch in the living room, and I took a seat there. "Fighting with one of your classmates..." My mom shook her head in disbelief. "I've never seen you act this way before. What has gotten into you?"

My tail lashed. "What has gotten into me? Oh, I don't know... maybe it has something to do with how I'm fed up with the way everyone looks at me—" I drew in a ragged breath, "Mom, why didn't you tell me I can do magic? I felt its presence in your workshop and in the woods. It's magic! I *know* it is!"

My mother blinked and glanced away. "Lesley, please. I'm only trying to protect you."

"Oh, sure. You just want to protect me. What about protecting me from all the bullying at school? Why not let me learn how to... to change back into a normal girl?"

"Is that what this is about?" She reached out, gently laying a hand on my shoulder. "Sweetie, even if I knew such a spell, I can't teach you magic."

I shrugged her hand away. "And why is that, exactly?"

"Because to a cambion, magic can be addictive."

I blinked. "What?"

"You might become so obsessed with the power that it drives you insane. I don't want that to happen to you."

I remained silent for a long moment. "But... but it doesn't *always* happen, does it?"

She bit her lip, looking away.

"We'll be careful," I pleaded. "You can guide me every step of the way, and we'll both make sure that doesn't happen. Please! There must be some way to hide my horns and tail and wings!"

My mother only shook her head, her gaze on the floor. "It's too risky. I couldn't—"

"You know what?" I snapped. "I'd rather get driven insane by magic than continue on as a *freak*!" I stomped down the hallway to my room. Slamming the door, I collapsed onto my bed, wrapping my wings around myself. I hid my face in my hands as tears trickled.

For a while, I just sat there, cocooned within my wings. Finally, I turned my gaze toward my dresser. I crept over and pulled the bottom drawer. There, hidden among my old books and toys, was the wooden jewelry box. I lifted the lid and peered inside at the tattered scroll and the gold necklace, letting the calm I felt from the scarlet jewel wash over me.

9

The Festival

The next week at school, I strode along the hall, my tail swishing nervously. Through the crowd of students, I saw Zack by his locker. I swallowed and stepped up to him. "Hey, Zack?"

He turned. "Oh, hi, Lesley."

I hesitated. "Uh, see you at lunch today?"

"Of course," he said. "I never sit anywhere else, do I?"

"All right then." I smiled, but after I turned away, my expression soured. *Real smooth, Lesley,* I thought as I trudged through the crowd. I rounded a corner and approached Sadie's locker. She looked up from loading her backpack. "Lesley? What's the matter?"

I took a breath. "I, uh, I wanted to find out if you and Jeremy were going to the Samhain festival tonight."

Sadie zipped up her backpack. "Well, Jeremy will be at the festival, but he'll be playing in the Faeball game. He joined the team this year. Isn't that cool? He's finally taking some initiative." She paused. "As for me going... I'm not sure. I don't like all the noise." Sadie crooked an eyebrow at me. "Why do you ask?"

I swallowed. "Well, I wanted to ask Zack to come with me, but then I thought I should find out if anyone else was going so that it's not just me and Zack, so that it wouldn't seem like—"

"A date?" Sadie smirked. "Why would that be a problem? You don't have a crush on him or something, do you?"

I blinked. "Uh…"

"Come on, don't you know anything about vampires? My hearing is sensitive enough to detect heartbeats, including the way yours changes when Zack is around." She glanced behind me. "And even if I couldn't, the way your tail twitches is a dead giveaway."

I stilled the swaying of my tail. "Wait a second… you *knew*! You've known how I feel about Zack this whole time, haven't you?"

Sadie smirked. "Only since the day Murk stole his glasses."

"Oh, *only* since then?" I rolled my eyes. I paused, lowering my voice. "But… Sadie, there's another reason I want someone to come with me. Supposedly, Nerissa will be going to a 'secret meeting' at the festival. I want to try and follow her, but I would feel safer if someone else was with me. So won't you come to the festival tonight with me and Zack? Please?"

"All right. I'll go with you, but only on one condition."

"Okay, deal. What is it?"

"Get me some earplugs."

* * *

Zack and Sadie followed on either side of me as we stepped along the forest path. Jack-o'-lanterns lined both sides of the trail, casting flickering light across the fallen leaves. Through the trees to the west, the crimson glow of twilight was fading. There was a chill in the air, but it wasn't unpleasant. It stirred my blood, making me feel more alert.

Silence hung heavily over the woods, like the entire forest was holding its breath in anticipation. I stepped carefully over the carpet of leaves, not wanting to disturb the calm.

I glanced at the festively carved pumpkins. "Back where I'm from, we call today Halloween. People—humans, I mean—celebrate it by dressing up as witches and devils and vampires and things."

Sadie smirked. "I know. But how to you know that some of the 'costumes' being worn tonight aren't actually fae just being themselves?"

"Halloween always seemed silly to me," Zack murmured. A moment later, he chuckled. "But yeah, I bet either of you could win a costume contest."

I smiled at Zack, my cheeks reddening from something other than the autumn chill.

Up ahead, a wrought-iron gate opened through a weathered brick wall. The wall enclosed a small park-like area in the middle of the woods with a pond in the center. I led the way as we stepped through the gate. As I gazed into the calm water, a sense of peace washed over me. This wasn't just any pond. It was the wellspring of Misty Hollow, the town's source of magic. Somewhere under my feet, one of Yggdrasil's roots was drinking from the spring, drawing in the magic and opening the way into the Sacred Grove.

A pair of dryads, dressed in park ranger uniforms and holding rune-carved walking sticks, stood guard at another gate on the far side. Both were women, one not much older than me. "Be safe, and stay on the path," one of the dryads said as we passed through the gate.

More jack-o'-lanterns lined the trail, and every so often, we passed another dryad standing guard. In the distance, I saw the light of bonfires flickering. Soon, the silence of the forest gave way to jubilant singing and laughter.

Dozens of bonfires dotted an open field, roaring amid rows of tents, pavilions, and market stands. Crowds milled about, lining up to buy things, feasting at tables laden with food, or gathering around to musical performances. Fae from havens all across the world had come here tonight. Elves and witches in street clothes mingled with kitsune in colorful kimonos, kaftar in desert robes, and kinnara in bejeweled dresses. I grinned at the variety on display.

Sadie had the opposite reaction. Frowning, she took a pair of foam cylinders from her purse and stuck them in her ears. A moment later, she relaxed. "Oh, that's much better."

"You'll be okay with those?" I asked.

"Yes, I think so."

Nearby, a group of satyrs danced and played music. The musicians stomped their hooves as they played flutes and panpipes, while the dancers swung from one another's arms, leaping over each other and into the air. I glanced out at the crowd again. Something was different about the fae tonight, something more than the festive atmosphere of Samhain.

"They're not as anxious," I murmured to myself. In Misty Hollow, everyone knew humans might show up unexpectedly, so they were constantly on the lookout, constantly a little on edge. But tonight, the fae were standing taller, laughing louder, smiling wider.

"This is how the fae used to live," Sadie said to me, "before the ebbing of magic. Back then—I'm talking, like, thousands of years ago—all of our territory was protected year-round as heavily as the festival is tonight."

I glanced toward the edge of the woods. Evenly spaced jack-o'-lanterns sat along the perimeter, enclosing the entire field as far as I could see. I had a feeling they weren't just decorative. "All this just to keep humans out?"

"Not just humans," Sadie said. "There are worse things lurking in the Sacred Grove."

"Like what?"

"Well, there are unfriendly spirits," Zack offered. "Feral werewolves, troll bandits…"

"Don't forget about zombies," Sadie added.

"Zombies?" I shivered.

"Oh, and of course, dragons," Zack finished.

"Seriously, *dragons*?" I narrowed my eyes. "Guys, are you messing with me right now?"

Zack smirked. "You wanted to track down Nerissa, right?" He glanced out into the crowd. "That may be a bit of a challenge."

I pointed to where we'd come in. "I was hoping to keep an eye on this spot and catch her when she gets here." I peered out at the festival again. "Hopefully, she hasn't arrived already."

I lingered near the path as Zack and Sadie explored nearby. Thankfully, it wasn't long before Nerissa emerged from the forest path. I followed her at a distance. The elf-girl ignored the festivities and glanced over her shoulder a lot. She was definitely up to something.

She ducked behind one of the tents next to the line of jack-o'-lanterns. I tiptoed after her and peeked around. Nerissa pulled a couple things from her purse. One was a small pouch, while the other was the carved wooden stick I'd seen before—a magic wand. She sprinkled the contents of the pouch on the ground between two of the pumpkins and waved the wand through the air above them.

The air rippled like heat rising above a hot stove. It was like an invisible curtain hung above the line of pumpkins, and whatever Nerissa was doing was revealing it. A hole appeared in the veil of distorted air, just large enough for her to step through, which she quickly did. She turned, and with another wave of her wand, the hole closed. When it did, Nerissa was gone.

It's concealing magic, meant to hide this place from the outside. I guess it works both ways. I hesitated before creeping behind the tent, hoping I was just as invisible to Nerissa as she was to me. In the darkness, I couldn't tell what she'd sprinkled on the ground. Reaching out above the line of jack-o'-lanterns, I gasped as my fingertips vanished amid wavering distortions. I pulled my hand back in surprise before reaching out again, watching as my arm disappeared into the curtain of shimmering air.

"What are you doing?" a voice snapped. I turned. It was a dryad—and not just any dryad, but the red-haired elf who'd found me after I got lost in the woods. She narrowed her eyes. "You again?"

I jerked my arm back. "I just saw someone sneak out through here."

"I don't think so. I would have sensed it liked I sensed you just now."

"She cast a spell."

"Oh, really?" She rolled her eyes. "Come away from there."

"But—"

The dryad grabbed me by the wrist, dragging me back around the tent. She shot a warning look at me before continuing her patrol. Huffing a sigh, I took out my phone and called Sadie to find out where she and Zack had gone.

"Did you find Nerissa?" Sadie asked once I'd caught up with them.

"Yes, but she got away. I saw her sneak out through the ward."

She raised an eyebrow. "Without being detected?"

"Yeah. She cast some kind of spell to make a hole in it." I shivered. "What is she doing out there?"

"The spirits are out tonight," Zack said. "She could be meeting with one of them."

"If Nerissa was able to sneak through the ward..." Sadie's brow furrowed with worry. "I don't know. Maybe it's a better idea if we just steer clear of her."

"It sounds like there isn't much you can do anyway," Zack said. "I say just forget about Nerissa for tonight." He smiled. "Let's enjoy the festivities. Come on, Sadie tells me Jeremy is playing in the Faeball game."

* * *

Around us, the crowd murmured. Sets of wooden bleachers, which appeared to have been assembled from roughly hewn logs, encircled a grassy field. I sat next to Sadie in the highest row of the bleachers. On the field below, two teams stood poised for action. One wore jerseys of green and white, the colors of Misty Hollow High School, while the other team wore black and gold. All of them had colored flags clipped to their belts—gold for the opposing team, green for Misty Hollow.

"Who are we playing against?" I asked Sadie.

She removed a foam cylinder from one of her ears. "What was that?"

I repeated my questioned, and Sadie peered out at the field below. "I think the other team is from Pinnacle High School. Pinnacle is a haven out on the west coast."

"The west coast? It's hard to believe they just *walked* all the way here."

Between the two teams, a pair of glassy orbs sat on the ground. Each was at least three feet across and must have weighed hundreds of pounds. Veins of crystal inside each orb glowed brightly. One orb glowed green for Misty Hollow, the other gold for Pinnacle. Lines had been chalked across the grass like yard-lines on a football field. The orbs were about twenty yards apart, and each team was lined up behind their crystalline orb.

"What are those for?" I asked, pointing at the glassy spheres.

"They indicate what portion of the field each team controls," Sadie explained.

A centaur at the front of the Pinnacle team held a ball that glowed bright gold. A shaggy, wolfish Jeremy faced him, crouched down on his paws, his ears laid back. Jeremy seemed nervous. The granite colored troll stood next to him—easily the tallest player on the field. The troll glanced over at Jeremy, nodding to him. After a pause, Jeremy nodded back.

A whistle blew, and the teams charged forward. The centaur galloped past Jeremy. The werewolf spun, looking this way and that, appearing to have lost track of his opponent. Finally, he gave chase. A warlock riding a broomstick skimmed ahead of him, catching up to the centaur before Jeremy could. The warlock snatched for the flag clipped to his opponent's flank, but the centaur dodged.

Jeremy grunted as he chased down the centaur, kicking up clods of dirt with his claws. The centaur was about to reach the end zone, but Jeremy lunged, reaching out and unhooking the centaur's flag. Another whistle was blown, and everyone stopped. In the stands, the crowd around me cheered. Jeremy looked down at the flag in his claws and around at his cheering teammates, his eyes wide with surprise. He threw back his head and released a triumphant howl.

I didn't notice until that moment something else had been happening on the field. The troll had been pushing one of the crystal orbs. He had stopped along with everyone else, but the orb rolled a few inches further, crossing the line on which the other orb lay. The glow from the orbs flickered, and they switched colors. More cheers erupted from the crowd.

From the foot of the bleachers, Zack had been watching the field. He turned and climbed the steps to where Sadie and I sat. "Here you go," Zack said, smiling as he handed me a cup of cola.

I took a sip and smiled back. "Thanks."

"Yeah," Sadie said. "I would have asked you to get me something too, but… you know…"

I rolled my eyes at her before turning to Zack again. "What do you think of the game?"

"It's interesting. I like how each team member has to contribute something different." His eyes glimmered in the light of the distant bonfires. "I'm glad you invited me."

I didn't know if it was because of the festivities or the protection of the wards or because of the magic that filled the Sacred Grove, but that night, I felt really comfortable around Zack. And he was right. I should forget about Nerissa and just enjoy the moment. I scooted a little closer to him.

The teams lined up again, this time nose to nose, since there was hardly any distance between the orbs. The centaur held the ball in his hands, glaring into Jeremy's eyes. This time, Jeremy didn't look quite as nervous. The whistle blew.

Jeremy dodged to the side. The centaur galloped past him, kicking up clods of dirt. The warlock swooped in from behind and snatched the ball out of the centaur's hands. The

94

centaur chased after him, reaching for his flag, but the warlock stayed just out of reach. He scrunched his brow in concentration and moved his lips, reciting a spell. The ball flickered and flashed. Finally, its glow changed from gold to green, and the warlock flung the ball toward Jeremy. The wolf-boy reached out, catching the ball as he dove into the end zone. Around me, the crowd roared with applause. "Yeah, go Jeremy!" I cheered.

Once the crowd quieted down again, I inched closer to Zack. "So, how are you liking life in Misty Hollow now?"

"Just fine," he said. "I'm finally getting used to everything."

I glanced away bashfully. "Does that include getting used to a certain half-demon girl?"

He tilted his head at me. "What do you mean?"

I chewed my lip. "Zack—"

My cup jumped out of my hands. I yelped as the lid exploded off, splashing cola in my face and spilling it down the front of my shirt.

Sadie's eyes widened. "Lesley!" She stood up and dug inside her purse for a handkerchief.

"What happened?" Zack exclaimed, also rising from his seat.

I sat there helplessly, blinking fizzy drops out of my eyes.

"Come on, let's get you home," said Sadie, taking me by the arm.

She and Zack helped me to my feet, and the three of us headed down from the bleachers. As we did, I saw Nerissa watching me through the crowd. Her hand was closed around something. She sneered at me as she slipped the carved wooden wand back inside her purse.

10

The Labyrinth

A few days later, I rolled my bike to a stop in front of the flower shop. My mom was behind the cash register, helping someone buy a bouquet of roses. The customer—an elf with long, blond hair and dashing looks—nodded to my mother in thanks. He was about to leave, but turned to her again. "I'm wondering... have we met before? You look familiar somehow."

"I only started working here a couple months ago," my mom said.

The elf shrugged and turned to leave. But when he saw me, his eyes widened. He spun to face my mother. "Wait a minute... Jane Robinson? We used to go to school together. You're that witch who..." He glanced at me again. "Good day," he said curtly to my mom, hurrying out of the store.

I chewed my lip. "Sorry. Maybe I shouldn't come here anymore."

"It's okay, sweetie." My mom gave me a smile. "Did you need something?"

"No. I was just on my way to Sadie's house, and I thought I'd stop in here for a minute, but..." I shook my head. "Your boss won't be happy if I'm scaring away customers like that. We can talk later."

I said goodbye to my mom and pedaled my bike to the street shrouded by overhanging branches. Once I was through the gate in front of Sadie's house, I laid my bike next to two others on the lawn. Inside, Jeremy and Zack sat with Sadie in the parlor. The glassy-eyed butler, Rupert, offered me a tray of store-bought cookies. I took one and sat down. "Hey guys."

Our conversation soon turned to what had happened a few nights ago at the festival. "Yeah, I saw you up in the stands all soaking wet," Jeremy said. "You're sure Nerissa did it by casting a spell?"

"It was her all right," I said. "She has a magic wand."

"Have you told the principal?" Sadie asked.

"Why even bother? You know Principal Constance isn't going to believe me." I paused. "What we need is proof. We should investigate."

Zack glanced at Rupert, who stood motionless by the kitchen door. "Should we be talking about this in front of him?"

"It's probably fine," Sadie said. "Rupert can't speak, and I'm not sure he really understands us. He seems to respond mostly to mesmerism."

"Just in case, could you send him away?"

"Sure." Sadie rose and faced the butler. She peered into his eyes, her brow scrunched in concentration. After a moment, Rupert turned and marched upstairs.

Sadie returned to her chair. As she did, she looked at me. "What?"

I grinned. "That's *so* cool that you can do that."

She shrugged. "It comes with being a vampire."

Zack gave her a wary glance. "That only works on the undead, right?"

Sadie smirked. "Wanna look into my eyes and find out?" She chuckled at his startled expression. "You're perfectly safe, Zack. I'm not skilled enough to mesmerize something with a mind of its own." She giggled. "Oh! I should tell you about the time Lesley first came over."

I blushed. "Please don't."

Zack cleared his throat. "Back to what we were talking about before. I think Lesley is right. Whose side do you think the principal is gonna take? We need proof of what Nerissa is doing."

Jeremy glanced between me and Zack. "If you do investigate Nerissa or whatever, leave me out of it. I don't want to get into any more trouble."

"I understand, Jeremy." I turned. "How about you, Sadie?"

She frowned, uncertain. "I guess it wouldn't hurt to at least keep an eye on Nerissa."

* * *

Not even two days later, I had another incident, this time at the library.

I looked up from my notebook. The room was quiet except for the occasional whisper or the rustle of a page being turned. Through the windows, the sky was taking on a gold tinge as the sun sank to the west. Across the table from me, Zack was hunched over his homework. Sadie sat between us, scanning over the pages of her textbook with unblinking eyes. Even after two hours of studying, she showed no signs of fatigue. *I guess there are some advantages to being undead.* At one of the other tables, Nerissa sat with her gossamer-winged friend Daphne, also doing homework.

I sat back in my chair and sighed. "Well, I've had enough of this. Who wants to go exploring?"

"I could use a break," said Zack, pushing aside his textbook.

"I'm good," said Sadie. "You two go ahead." She winked at me.

I rolled my eyes at her. "Come on," I said to Zack.

The aisle stretched out before us. With each step we took, the bookshelves loomed higher. After some twists and turns, the path widened until it seemed we were on a city street, surrounded by tall buildings. Except the buildings were constructed of bookshelves or were nothing more than stacks of enormous books. The library's ceiling—looming impossibly high above us—seemed painted with blue and white patterns mimicking clouds and sky. Rows of potted plants lined the aisle, but they stood as tall as the trees along a city boulevard.

"There's no one else here, you know," Zack said to me.

My insides fluttered. "What?"

"You don't have to keep your wings folded so tight like that," Zack said. "No one else is going to see them."

"Oh. Yeah, I guess you're right." I let my wings unfurl, flapping them a few times. "That is a bit more comfortable. Thanks."

"I've been wondering something. Since you've got wings, can you fly?"

"My mom says I should be able to, but I've never really tried." I reached out to the side and stretched one of the webbed appendages to its full length. The fringe of my wing extended at least twelve inches past my fingertips. "Maybe someday I will, though. At least there's something good about these freakish things I can look forward to."

Zack watched me for a moment. "Don't say that about your wings. They're not freakish."

My cheeks warmed. *So you don't think I'm ugly after all?* I wanted to ask. "Uh, thanks." I said instead. I turned away to hide my blushing, but pretended I was peering along the street. Ahead, between two of the book-buildings, was a park filled with white-leafed trees. I pointed. "How about that way?"

The two of us headed into the park. We passed into the shade of the trees, and I realized the leaves rustling in the breeze were actually the pages of books. Something fluttered past my face. I laughed when I saw it was an origami butterfly folded from a printed page. Zack smiled as he reached out his hand, and the paper butterfly alighted on his extended finger.

Then both of us jumped as thunder rang out. I looked up at a sky that was suddenly filled with billowing, gray clouds. Zack squinted at the threatening sky as rain pattered around us.

He looked at me. "Time to go back?"

I nodded. "Yeah, let's get out of here." I closed my eyes, imagining myself back at the Misty Hollow Public Library. But when I opened them again, I was still in the fantastical park beneath the book-trees.

And Zack was gone.

Pages drifted down from the branches above. I closed my eyes and tried to clear my mind again, but when I looked around, I was still stuck. The rain was falling harder, and the wind was picking up. The branches of the trees swayed and rattled, scattering their pages in a flurry around me. Not knowing what else to do, I turned and ran back the way I had come, hoping to find my way back through the maze of bookshelves.

The floor sloped downward. Soon, I was clambering down a steep staircase made of giant, stacked books. Icy rain spattered me. I held up one of my wings against the rain. "Help!" I cried. My voice echoed back through the fog.

Lightning cracked, and thunder boomed. I ran, scrambling down the slope. When I looked around again, I was somehow at the bottom of a narrow canyon. Bookshelves loomed on either side of me like craggy cliffs. Water was rushing along the ground, splashing over the tops of my shoes.

I pressed my hands to my temples and closed my eyes, trying to snap out of it. But when I looked again, I was still trapped in the canyon beneath the driving rain and flashing lightning. The water was rising steadily, the current tugging at my ankles. I turned, but the staircase I had come down was gone. I glanced back at my wings—now would be a *really* good time for me to learn to fly. I spread them and tried to flap, but they only caught the wind, which nearly knocked me over. Folding my wings again, I clambered up one of the shelves, knocking books into the water with each step.

Another boom rang through the canyon. I peered up at the book-lined cliffs and wiped raindrops from my eyes. Below me, soaked pages were floating in the raging current. The water was still rising. "Help!" I climbed onto another shelf as the flood swallowed the one below.

I realized the low, rhythmic booming I heard wasn't thunder. Eyes wide, I peered out into the storm. Lightning flashed, and I shuddered when I saw something silhouetted inside the clouds. The huge shape drew nearer, the flapping of its wings echoing like thunder from the canyon walls. It swooped down out of the clouds. The massive reptile was covered in black scales that glistened wetly in the rain. The dragon turned its head toward me and opened its mouth, breathing a stream of fire. With a yelp, I leaped. The shelf I had been standing on a moment ago was engulfed in flames.

My wings flapped instinctively, clawing desperately at the air, but the wind knocked me off balance. Screaming, I fell toward the churning water and plunged into the freezing current. Shivers racked my body as the cold waves splashed over me. I swam for the edge, gasping for air as I did, and clung to a toppled bookshelf with numb fingers.

Above me, the dragon opened its jaws again. Then a voice called out. "Hey! Over here!"

I turned and saw the bespectacled librarian hovering in the air, her butterfly wings thrumming rapidly. In her hand was a magic wand. She swung the wand, launching a shooting star that trailed glittering sparks, and the projectile slammed into the side of the dragon's head. The monster turned away from me, bellowing with rage as the fairy woman launched another meteor of starry sparks.

The dragon flapped toward the librarian and sent a stream of fire in her direction. The fairy's wings blurred as she dodged the flames. As the beast drew closer, the librarian wove her wand in a complicated series of motions, tracing out a glowing rune in the air. Lightning crackled, and the shelf I was clinging to shook. Moments later, I lost my grip. A scream bubbled from my throat as I was dragged beneath the icy water.

But I realized I wasn't drowning. In fact, I was completely dry. I opened my eyes and found myself sprawled on the carpeted floor of the library, clutching the base of one of the bookshelves. I clambered to my feet. The librarian stood next to me, her wand still in hand as she continued to weave it through the air.

I gasped. A funnel of storm clouds was streaming down into the pages of a book that lay open on the floor. In the middle of the vortex, the dragon was flapping hard, fighting to escape. It was tiny now and growing smaller by the second. It bellowed, breathing a stream of fire, but the flames were sucked down into the swirling funnel. Finally, the dragon itself was swallowed up, and the cover of the book—a hardback copy of *Harry Potter and the Goblet of Fire*—slammed shut.

The librarian breathed a sigh. She slipped her wand inside her vest and placed the book back on the shelf. She turned to me. "Are you all right?"

I dusted myself off. "I think so. What happened?"

"Someone must have broken one of the magical seals," the fairy explained. "No doubt they thought it would be funny, whoever did it. But you could have been hurt. You're sure you're okay?"

I nodded and turned toward the entrance to the aisle. Zack peeked his head around the corner. "Lesley! There you are!"

A moment later, Sadie peered in. "We heard a noise. Did something happen?"

I looked past my friends to the table where Daphne and Nerissa were sitting. "Yeah," I muttered, "and I think I know who's responsible."

The three of us strode over to the table. I crossed my arms. "Hey, Riss."

Nerissa sneered at me. "What's the matter, Lesley? Did something happen to you inside the Labyrinth?"

"I think you know very well what just happened. And I think it's got something to do with the magic wand you have in your purse." I tried to snatch her purse, which lay on the table next to her backpack.

She grabbed the purse before I could. "What, in here?" She held the purse open for me to see. The carved wooden wand wasn't inside.

I blinked. "But at the festival, I saw—"

"Ooh, then maybe I did it by sprinkling some magic herbs," Nerissa said. "But even if you tell the principal that I—let's just say—tampered with the library's magical seals with the intent of unleashing something on you, well... it's your word against mine. Tell me, Lesley, which of us is she going to believe? A prim and proper elf like me or a *freak* like you?" She slung her purse over her shoulder and picked up her backpack, and she and Daphne strode out of the library.

I stared blankly at the entrance after Nerissa and her friend had left. Slowly, I turned to Sadie and Zack. "Oh. My. God! Did you hear what she just said? She basically admitted to it!"

"She's right, though," Sadie said. "Without evidence, the principal isn't going to listen to you. We should—"

"We should get back at her," I snapped. "*That's* what we should do!"

Sadie's eyes widened. "No! That will only make things worse."

I crossed my arms. "I am the daughter of a witch. It is traditional among witches to settle disputes by the casting of hexes."

She looked desperately at Zack. "Talk some sense into her, please."

"Sorry, Sadie," Zack said, "but I'm with Lesley on this one. We ought to give Nerissa a taste of her own medicine."

"Do you guys know where that ruined cabin in the woods is?" I asked. "Let's meet there on Friday night, say, at eleven o'clock. In the meantime, I'll find out what sort of hexes are in my mom's spellbook and what ingredients they need." I looked at Sadie. "Are you coming or not?"

Her shoulders sagged. "Fine," Sadie grumbled. "I'll come along, but only to keep an eye on you."

11

Hexed

The house was completely quiet. Moonlight streamed in through my window blinds. I crept out of bed and quickly got dressed, tucking my satchel under my arm. I held my breath as I tiptoed along the hallway past my mother's bedroom. When I reached the kitchen, I stopped when I saw Rugby sprawled in the middle of the floor. His eyes were closed, his breath wheezing in and out through his nostrils. I hadn't been expecting this—Rugby usually slept at the foot of my mom's bed. I hesitated and edged my way around the kitchen, past the sleeping dog. I was halfway around when the floor creaked beneath my feet. My heart hammered. I tried to hold completely still but couldn't keep my tail from swishing.

Rugby didn't stir. Silently releasing a breath, I crept the rest of the way around and opened the back door, stepping out into the night.

Stars shimmered in the sky, and the rising moon floated just above the treetops. My breath fogged in the cold air. I stepped across the lawn toward the old shed beneath the willow tree. I knelt and unzipped my satchel. "Desperate times," I told myself, taking out the gold necklace and the scroll of spells. I clasped the amulet's chain around my neck, and a sense of focus poured into me. I turned my gaze to the door and read the unlocking spell.

The latch clicked, and the door creaked open. I smiled as a shiver of delight ran through me. Then I frowned down at the necklace. I took it off and stuffed it and the scroll back inside my satchel and pulled out a flashlight. Inside the shed, my mother's spellbook was lying open on her workbench, surrounded by jars of ingredients and half-melted candles. Under my flashlight beam, I flipped through the pages until I found the first spell I'd looked at the night before. I scanned over the lists of ingredients and peered at the labels of various bottles and jars, collecting some of them into my satchel. Finally, I took the spellbook and crept back outside.

I hurried down the street to where a trail led into the woods. I followed the path, navigating the twists and turns, until I emerged into a small clearing. The solitary chimney of the ruined cabin loomed black against the sky. I checked the time on my phone—it was almost eleven.

"Hey," I whispered. "Guys? Anyone else here?"

"Boo!" Zack jumped out from behind the chimney.

I shuddered. "Zack!"

He chuckled and looked around. "Is Sadie here yet?"

"Over here, guys." Sadie stepped into the clearing. "It wasn't easy for me to sneak out, so this had better be worth it."

I led them over to the stone floor of the ruined cabin, and we sat in a circle, facing one another. I took the spellbook from my satchel, along with the jars of ingredients, and set up and lit some candles.

Between us, golden flames flickered, dancing in the chill breeze. I set a bronze bowl next to the book and placed a bundle of dried herbs in it. "All right, guys," I said. "To start,

I figure we should test things out." I flipped through the spellbook's dog-eared pages. "This spell is supposed to summon a kind of spirit called a 'familiar.' If it works, the spirit can help us cast the hex." I handed Zack the bowl with the herbs. "Here, wave this around slowly."

"Like this?" Zack held out the brass bowl, gently moving it in circles.

"Yes, exactly. Now, Sadie, do the same with one of the candles."

"Okay..." She peered dubiously at a candle next to her, carefully picked it up, and moved it slowly back and forth while shielding its flame with her other hand.

I took a breath. "All right. Now for the incantation." I peered down at the spellbook.

Spirits of this place, hear me!
On this night I seek your aid.
You haven't any need to fear me.
Accept these gifts I have here laid.
Spirits of this place, hear me!
I seek your guidance on this night.
Don't be afraid, but come near me.
Accept this offering of light.

We waited in silence for a minute, but nothing happened.

"Do you think it worked?" I whispered.

"Is a familiar spirit supposed to show up?" Zack looked around, "I don't see any—"

Somewhere up in the trees, an owl hooted.

"Maybe that's it," I whispered. "Familiars are supposed to take the form of animals."

Sadie set down her candle. "Or maybe it's just an owl?"

I cleared my throat. "Uh, Mr. Owl, will you help us cast a spell?"

The owl hooted again.

"There, see?" Zack said to Sadie.

She rolled her eyes. "It's just an *owl*, for goodness' sake." She shook her head. "Whatever. Let's just get this over with."

I turned through the pages of the spellbook. "Zack, gimme that bowl." I took out the bundle of herbs, frowned at it, then tossed the herbs into the trees toward where the owl had hooted. I set the bowl down and added some oil and crushed herbs. Finally, I reached into my pocket and pulled out a small, tangled knot of blond hair, setting it on top of everything.

"Is that Nerissa's hair?" Sadie asked. "How did you manage to get that?"

"I stole—I mean *borrowed*—her hairbrush." I glanced toward the trees. "All right, Mr. Owl—assuming you're actually a familiar spirit who can understand us—here goes." I drew in a breath.

Let she who torments me despair!
Let her, through this lock of hair,
Come to understand my pain,
And never torment me again!

I touched the flame of one of the candles to the pile of stuff in the bowl, and it all went up in a burst of green fire. Smoke billowed, carrying with it the stench of burning hair. Zack coughed. He stood up, backing away from the smoking bowl. I likewise retreated from the stench.

Sadie got up. "Well, okay then." She turned to me. "How do we know if the spell worked?"

I rubbed at my eyes. "I don't know," I said, coughing. "I guess we'll wait and see."

* * *

On Monday the next week, I was at my locker, putting away some books, when Sadie came up to me. She held out a piece of paper. The words *Talent Show Sign Up* were printed across the top. "I just remembered the talent show is coming up in a few weeks," Sadie explained.

"Cool," I said. "You're gonna sign up?"

"I want to sign us *both* up. You play guitar, right? You can accompany me."

I hesitated. "I don't know. I'm not actually that good at guitar."

"That's why we'll practice first. We've got plenty of time." She blinked puppy-dog eyes at me. "Come on. You're not gonna make me go up in front of the school and sing all by myself, are you?"

I couldn't say no to that. "Actually, that does sound kind of fun."

We headed to the cafeteria. Peering through the crowd, I saw Pauline and Daphne at their usual table. Nerissa wasn't with them. I paused before heading over. "Hey guys. Have you seen Riss? She wasn't in history class today."

Pauline looked up at me. "Nerissa is sick today. She stayed home."

"She's sick?"

"Yeah, she's been sick all weekend." The centaur frowned at me. "Why do you care, freak?"

I ignored her unfriendly tone. "I was just wondering. Gosh, I hope she gets better soon." I headed to my usual table. "Zack, you'll never believe this. Nerissa has been sick all weekend! Ever since…"

Jeremy blinked, glancing between us. "Oh no, what did you guys do?"

"We cast a hex on her," said Zack.

Sadie looked surprise. "Wait, the spell actually worked?"

I stared down at the table. "I guess it did."

"Oh my god, how sick is Nerissa?" asked Sadie.

"I don't know. Pauline didn't say." I blew out a breath. "I didn't realize the hex would make her sick for so long."

Sadie placed a hand atop mine. "We really shouldn't be messing with magic to begin with."

I hated that she was right. Worse, I knew this was just what my mom had warned me about. "You're right. Maybe putting a hex on her was going too far." I looked at the others. "Yeah, no more of this. No more hexes, and"—I hesitated—"and no more magic."

But I wasn't sure I could keep that promise.

* * *

I was almost relieved when I saw Nerissa in history class the next day. She looked a little pale but otherwise was acting like her usual self. She stuck her tongue out at me as I passed by her desk.

Toward the end of the lesson, she was fidgeting with something inside her backpack. She glanced back at me, silently moving her lips. I shot a glare back at her, reconsidering how I felt about seeing her.

The bell rang, and my classmates rose from their desks. I packed up my satchel and tried to get up but blinked in confusion when I couldn't.

Nerissa stepped over to my desk. "Having trouble with something, Lesley?"

"Um…" My thighs seemed glued to the seat. I looked around, hoping to ask for help, but the room was empty except for Nerissa and me. A knot formed in my stomach.

Nerissa leaned down, looking me in the eye. "I've heard that witches sometimes cast hexes to get back at each other. Your mom is a witch, right? Has she taught you any interesting spells lately?"

"My mom won't teach me witchcraft. She's afraid magic will corrupt me."

"Oh, so you did it behind her back? Wow!"

"What? No, that's silly." I glanced away. "I didn't cast a hex on you, Nerissa."

"Really? Look me in the eye and tell me that."

I pushed against the desk but still couldn't get up. Finally, I looked at her. "I didn't cast a hex on you," I mumbled.

Nerissa shook her head. "You're not very good at lying, are you?" She stepped back and took something from her backpack—the crude magic wand I'd seen her with before. I tensed as she pointed the wand at me.

I swallowed. "Okay, fine! I did it. I didn't realize how bad it would be, and I'm sorry."

"I don't want your apology." She waved the wand.

I braced myself. But all that happened was my thighs suddenly coming unstuck from the seat of the desk. I tumbled to the floor.

I clambered to my feet. Nerissa glanced back at me from the doorway. "Don't mess with me again, freak," she warned before stepping into the hall.

* * *

There was a knock at the front door. I opened it and smiled at Sadie. Like she always did on sunny days, she wore her hat and sunglasses and held her parasol above her head.

"Ready for music practice?" I asked. I stepped aside to let her in, but she hesitated.

Sadie cleared her throat. "May I come in?"

I blinked. "Oh, right. Vampires have to be invited in. Yes, Sadie, please come inside."

I set up a music stand in the living room while my mom closed the curtains over the front windows to make Sadie more comfortable. Soon, I was strumming my acoustic guitar while Sadie read from a printout of lyrics, singing in time with the notes I plucked. My mom sat on the couch, watching quietly. Rugby lay next to her, resting his head on her lap.

When we finished the song, my mother clapped. "Very good." She turned to Sadie. "I didn't know Tobias and Agatha had adopted a daughter. Last I'd heard, Tobias was investigating reports of missing livestock over in Brighton. Did he ever solve that mystery?"

"If I recall… yes, my father did catch the culprit that time," Sadie replied. "It turned out to be a vampire like he suspected."

"Are you talking about yourself, Sadie?"

My friend shook her head. "No. The one from Brighton didn't have a soul, and my father wasn't able to tame it, so it had to be put down. I was found by a member of the Slayers Guild."

"Oh no. I bet that was scary."

"Yeah, kinda." Sadie's gaze grew distant for a moment.

"The Slayers Guild?" I asked.

"Humans who hunt paranormal creatures," Sadie explained. "Fortunately for me, when the Slayer realized I still had a soul, he decided to, um, sell me to my parents. For a sizable amount, I'm told. I hope I've been worth it to them."

"I'm certain you have," my mother said.

"Sell you?" I asked. "Your parents bought you?"

Sadie shrugged. "More like they paid to get me away from the Slayer. I'm not complaining."

We played the song again, but about halfway through, I faltered and stopped. "Hold on, I messed up that part." I pointed to the sheet music. "Can we go back to—"

Rugby lifted his head at another knock at the door. He leaped up off the couch and raced into the foyer, barking and snarling. My mom's eyes widened a little. She rose from the couch, following the dog.

"Hush," she murmured, pushing Rugby aside. She hesitated a moment before opening the front door.

Rugby whimpered, scurrying away as a man in an old-fashioned suit stepped inside. "So good to see you again, Jane." Asmodeus removed his top hat and made it disappear in a puff of smoke.

"Asmodeus," my mother murmured. She sounded nervous. "It's still over a month until the winter solstice. What are you doing here?"

He gave her a look that might have been either a smile or a sneer. "Just checking in." He glanced into the living room. His gaze slid past Sadie as if she wasn't even there, but when he looked at me, his eyes glowed with fire.

I shivered. Only a moment later did I notice that Sadie's eyes had gone wide with fright. The sheet of lyrics had slipped from her fingers and was fluttering to the floor.

"You're still planning on honoring our wager, aren't you?" Asmodeus said to my mother.

She glanced at me and swallowed. "Yes... yes, of course."

The demon prince smiled. He looked at me, and fire flashed in his eyes. "Remember, before midnight on the winter solstice." He conjured his hat and tipped it, disappearing out the front door.

Once he was gone, my mom let out a trembling sigh. I ran over to her and wrapped her in a hug. "Mom, it's okay."

Sadie could probably hear our hearts thumping from across the room. "Who was that?" she asked, her voice shaking.

My mother held me a moment longer before slipping out of the hug. "Just... an old colleague of mine," she said to Sadie. "I'm sorry if he frightened you."

Sadie glanced at the sheet of lyrics on the floor at her feet. "Terrified is a better word." She set the printout on the music stand. "I think I'm done for today."

I glanced warily at the front door. "Fine by me," I said with a shiver.

* * *

I did a lot of thinking that night because I sure didn't get much sleep after Asmodeus showed up like that. I had to do something. At school the next day, after classes had ended, I strode through the crowded halls. I rounded a corner and approached Sadie at her locker.

I swallowed. "I can't make it to music practice today. Something came up."

"Oh... okay," Sadie said. "See you tomorrow then."

I nodded and strode away down the hall before she could ask why my heart was beating so rapidly. I hurried to Zack's locker. "Hey, can we talk?"

115

Zack slung on his backpack. "Sure. What is it?"

"You know how I told Sadie 'no more magic'? I-I don't think I'll be able to keep that promise."

"Why is that?" He looked at me. "What's the matter?"

I glanced both ways over my shoulders. "I need your help."

The hallway slowly emptied out as my classmates headed home. Zack's eyes grew wider as I explained my situation with Asmodeus, telling him about the amulet the demon prince had given me. When I had finished, he blew out a breath. "This amulet lets you do *sorcery*?"

"Yes. I've only used it a few times, but... Zack, it feels like a part of me. Whenever I wear it, everything seems so clear." I chewed my lip. "I keep trying to tell myself Asmodeus's offer isn't tempting, but... it *is*. I'm ashamed I even feel this way, but I *am* tempted." I touched one of the horns on my brow. "He said I could learn to appear human again, and I want that more than anything!"

Zack watched me for a long moment. "What can I do to help?"

"Asmodeus's offer *can't* be my only option. There has to be another way. Maybe I can learn witchcraft instead of sorcery—hopefully that will satisfy the itch. Maybe I can even use witchcraft to shapeshift. Oh, god, I hope so."

"But you said your mom won't teach you."

"No, she won't, which means I need to find someone else to do it. Zack, you've gotten to know some of the other witches and warlocks in town. Do you know anyone who could?"

"You need someone who's willing to teach you witchcraft while keeping quiet about it." Zack nodded slowly. "Yeah. I think I know just the guy."

12

Cambion Blood

The warm sun fell across my spread wings, making up for the chill as I pedaled my bike along the street. I tilted my wings as I rounded a corner, my tail swaying behind me. It seemed so effortless to balance atop my bicycle with a subtle flexing of a wing, a slight tensing of a membrane, a gentle swish of my tail. *I really should try again at flying sometime.*

Fallen leaves skittered along the pavement as I rode past storefront windows. I passed by a bakery with its wonderful smell of cinnamon and apples and baking bread. Then I turned a corner onto a side street. The narrow lane—this one paved with bricks instead of asphalt—lay completely in the shade of the trees growing along it. I stopped in front of a small shop in the shadow of a huge, gnarled oak. Vines grew up along the building's front, their leaves turned brilliant red by the autumn chill. The shop had no windows, only a weathered wooden door. I propped my bike against the wall. A bell tinkled overhead as I stepped inside, into dimness and eerie, flickering candlelight.

It took a second for my eyes to adjust. Opposite the entrance, a counter ran along the back wall. Behind it stood

117

shelves stacked with bottles and jars filled with dried herbs and salts and preserved animal parts. At one end of the counter stood a set of brass scales and an old-fashioned cash register. The walls on either side of the store were lined with more shelves stacked with more jars as well as colorful crystals. Half-melted candles stood along the counter and in sconces on the walls. I blinked, almost startled to see that one of the candles stood atop a human skull, which was half covered in drips of melted wax.

From behind, I heard a rustle of feathers. A black shape fluttered toward me out of the shadows, its pointed beak gleaming in the candlelight. I yelped, holding my arms up in front of my face. Wingtips brushed against my wrist as the raven circled about, cawing menacingly.

The door behind the counter creaked open. "Ginger!" a voice snapped. "That's no way to treat a customer!"

The cawing and fluttering ceased. A man stood behind the counter. His forehead was lined with the wrinkles of decades of disapproving glares. The reflection of the candles seemed to flicker in his eyes, but I quickly realized it was actually the glimmer of witch-fire.

The man held out his arm, and the raven fluttered over to him, alighting on his wrist. "I'll have none of that from you," he chided the bird, wagging a finger at its beak. The man reached up to the shelves behind him, and the raven hopped off, perching on a piece of gnarled driftwood on the top shelf. He turned to me. "Terribly sorry about that," he began, but he tilted his head, taking a second look at me. "Ah, I see. Ginger didn't like the scent of your demonic blood."

I glanced up at the raven. It blinked a beady eye at me before burring its head beneath a wing. I turned to the man. "I'm looking for a warlock named Balthazar Crowley."

"You've found him." The man smiled, revealing a gold tooth among others that were crooked. "It's not often I'm visited by a cambion." He squinted at me. "Forgive me, but... you seem familiar somehow. Do I know you?"

"No, but you might know my mother. I'm Jane Robinson's daughter. My name is Lesley."

His eyes widened. "You're Jane's daughter? After all these years, she's come back to Misty Hollow?"

"Yes. You know my mother?"

Balthazar nodded. "She was one of my students. I used to teach at the high school, years ago before I retired. Jane was such a talented herbalist. I was disappointed to hear she'd been seduced by an incubus and ran away. I've always wondered what became of her." The warlock smoothed his expression. "Lesley, is it? Tell me, what brings you to my humble shop?"

"Mr. Crowley—"

"Please, call me Balthazar."

"Balthazar, I-I'm looking for someone to teach me how to do witchcraft."

"Oh, I'm sure your mother could—" He stopped. "She doesn't want you to learn magic, does she?"

I shook my head. "She's afraid I'll get corrupted by it. But what she doesn't understand, and what I'm afraid of, is that if I don't learn *something*, sooner or later I'll be lured into using... other kinds of magic."

The warlock paused. "You feel that magic is a part of you?"

"Yes!"

"Then indeed it may be just as dangerous to not teach you." He watched me for a moment. "But there's something more, isn't there?"

I reached up to touch my horns. "Yes. I want to appear human again."

His wrinkles bunched up as he furrowed his brow. "That may be possible, but shapeshifting is an advanced form of magic. It will likely take you years to learn."

"I don't care, so long as I'm working toward that goal. Will you teach me? Please?"

Balthazar let out a sigh. "If it is against your mother's wishes... No, I'm sorry, but I can't help you." He waved a hand, shooing me toward the exit. "Good day, Miss Robinson."

My eyes widened. "Wait! I can pay you."

He laughed. "Pay me? You're just a child. You wouldn't have enough money to—" He blinked, looking toward me again. "Unless..." He took a small vial from the shelf behind him, setting it down on the counter.

I leaned forward, peering at the vial. It was about half full of a thick, dark liquid. "What is it?"

"Cambion blood," the warlock explained. "It is a potent magical reagent, as valuable as it is rare, and as I'm sure you know, it's quite rare."

I shivered. "You want... some of my blood as payment?"

"That is the proposition, yes." Balthazar set the vial back on the shelf. "Give me a vial of your blood, and in exchange I will teach you witchcraft and, when you are skilled enough, help you learn shapeshifting."

I swallowed. "Fine... it's a deal."

He smiled, his gold tooth glinting. "Very well. This way, please." He motioned for me to step around the counter to the door leading to the back of the shop.

The shelves in the back room were stocked with even more jars and bottles. Some contained animal parts and organs floating in preserving fluid—one, I noticed with a shiver, contained extracted eyeballs. A desk stood in the corner, cluttered with ledgers and paperwork. Instead of lightbulbs, the office was lit by a pair of kerosene lanterns and a candle at one corner of the desk. I recalled my mom once saying that magic and electricity didn't get along.

From a desk drawer, Balthazar took a jar filled with some kind of greenish gel. "Rub this on your palm," he said, handing me the jar.

I removed the cork stopper, crinkling my nose as I sniffed the jar's contents. I dabbed some of the gel on my hand, smearing it across my palm. Wherever the gel touched my skin, it felt cool at first, then icy cold.

When I looked up again, I gave a start. Balthazar was holding a pocket knife. He passed the edge of the blade over the candle flame to sterilize it. He had set a strip of gauze and a small glass vial on the desk as well. The knife in his grip gleamed in the flickering lamplight.

He turned to me. "Hold out your hand," the warlock instructed.

I swallowed, then extended my open palm. I looked away, clenching my teeth. The warlock took my hand in his, and the knife sliced across my palm. It stung a little but didn't hurt as much as I had feared. The gel had numbed my skin.

I peeked at my hand. A shallow cut ran across my palm, red droplets beading up from it. Balthazar was holding the vial below the cut, waiting as my blood dripped into the vial. I shuddered, averting my eyes again. After a minute or so, Balthazar let go and wrapped gauze around my hand.

"The salve will ensure it heals quickly," he explained. The warlock held up the vial of my blood, smiling as he examined it under the lamplight.

He led me back to the main room, placing the vial on the shelf next to the other one. "I'll begin preparations for your first lesson. When I am ready, I will send for you."

I headed back through the shop. I peered down at my hand, rubbing at the gauze wrapped over the cut. As I stepped out through the front entrance, I heard Balthazar mutter, "I'm going to regret doing this, aren't I, Ginger?"

The raven cawed, seemingly in agreement.

* * *

A few days later, not long after I'd gotten home from school, Zack rolled his bicycle to a stop in front of the house. He waved to me as he walked up to the porch where I sat. I glanced at my palm, still amazed the cut was already completely healed—there wasn't even a scar. I raised my hand to wave back.

Rugby was lying on the porch next to me. As Zack approached, Rugby rose and growled.

"It's okay, Rugby," I said, tugging on his leash. "He's a friend." The dog looked at me, then at Zack again, and gave him a friendly sort of bark.

Zack peered cautiously at Rugby. "What's his problem?"

I shrugged. "He's weird sometimes. Rugby is actually..." I paused. "Rugby isn't what he appears to be."

Zack's wary look vanished as he smiled. "Oh, he's your mom's familiar spirit. Cool!"

I paused. "Uh, yeah, something like that."

Zack tentatively reached out. Rugby didn't growl, and Zack patted him between the ears. "Good doggy."

I glanced at the black-and-white dog. After Asmodeus's second appearance, my mom wanted to send Rugby along with me whenever I went out. She'd explained what Rugby really was and how he could protect me, and—I'll be honest—I was frightened at first. Even now, it was still hard for me to believe the puppy my mom had brought home when I was little was actually a creature she'd known since before I was born.

Rugby led the way as, side by side, Zack and I strolled through the neighborhood. I wanted to take Zack's hand in mine, but I still hadn't told him about my feelings for him. Besides, I had something else on my mind. We headed uphill, into the ritzy neighborhood, and passed by a cream-colored house. Another car was parked in the driveway next to Nerissa's silver convertible. When we reached the end of the block, I turned and led Rugby back the way we had come.

Zack gave me a look. "Are we spying on Nerissa?"

"Maybe."

We circled the block a couple of times, but I didn't see Nerissa anywhere. I was about to give up and head back when, from behind, I heard a door slam. I turned and saw Nerissa stomping out of her house, her fists clenched in anger. She hurried away down the sidewalk.

Zack and I gave each other surprised looks. We turned to follow Nerissa. I pulled Rugby's leash, tugging him along.

We kept our distance, trying to remain unnoticed. Once, we ducked behind a hedge when she glanced back, and twice, we nearly lost sight of her. Finally, Nerissa stepped off the sidewalk and into the bushes. We waited for a bit before following. The path led us downhill, into my neighborhood. We emerged onto the sidewalk, and I barely caught a glimpse of Nerissa as she rounded a corner half a block away. "I think I know where she's headed," I said to Zack.

We came to where the ditch ran through the culvert underneath the street. I looked at Zack, silently pressing a finger across my lips as I crept to the edge of the embankment. In the distance, the sound of footsteps crunched across gravel and splashed through shallow water.

I glanced at Zack, beckoning him to follow as I crept down the earthen slope into the ditch, pulling a reluctant Rugby after me. Zack followed as we crept along the creek bed.

"There." Zack pointed.

I followed his gaze, and saw Nerissa in the distance, her back turned as she strode along the ditch. We picked up our pace, following her.

The ditch widened out, and the stream's course began to meander. We had come past the edge of the neighborhood and were in the woods now. Wane sunlight seeped through the clouds, filtering down through the branches above.

Nerissa headed up the embankment, crunching across the forest's carpet of fallen leaves. She stopped, glancing back, and grabbed something from her purse and waved it in the air. A swirl of leaves burst up from the ground, surrounding her. When they settled, she was gone.

Giving up on stealth, I dashed along the creek bed. I stared down at the spot where Nerissa had vanished. There was only a spiral pattern in the leaf litter.

Rugby sniffed at the spot on the ground. Zack came up behind. "Did you see that?" he murmured in astonishment.

"Now how are we supposed to find her?" I asked.

He paused. "We could split up."

"I don't know... that never seems to work in the movies."

Zack paused for a moment. "We'll cover more ground that way. Besides, you've got Rugby to protect you." He turned, heading off into the trees.

I hesitated before turning the other direction. I crept slowly across the fallen leaves, trying not to crunch through them too loudly. I peered out among the gnarled boughs, my tail swishing. Rugby sniffed the ground, but every so often, he whimpered at me with worry.

A few minutes later, Zack called out. "Lesley!"

He sounded frightened. "Zack!" Rugby didn't protest as I ran through the trees, the dog bounding alongside me.

I stopped and ducked behind a trunk. A shadowy figure stood among the trees. I couldn't see who it was because they were draped in a black, hooded cloak and had their back turned. The figure glanced this way and that, as if looking around in alarm. A leather-bound spellbook and an animal skull surrounded by half-melted candles lay in the hollow of a nearby tree. At the figure's feet, a summoning circle was traced in the mud. As the figure looked about, a necklace swung from around their neck. A shining, blood red jewel dangled from the gold chain. The jewel was shaped differently than the one on my necklace, but there was no mistaking it for another enchanted amulet containing the power of sorcery.

Rugby was crouched behind me. Fortunately, he was smart enough to keep quiet, but he tugged the leash back in the direction we'd come. It seemed like a good suggestion. I followed as Rugby slunk through the forest, stepping carefully to make as little noise as possible. A minute later, I glanced back. No one seemed to be following.

I jumped as my phone buzzed inside my pocket. I answered and heard the sound of heavy breathing over the connection. "Lesley, where are you?" Zack said between gasps. "Are you okay?"

"I'm fine," I whispered, still glancing around warily. "What happened?"

"I saw someone wearing a black robe," Zack explained. "It was creepy. I ran as fast as I could."

"I saw them too."

"You got away okay?"

"Yeah." I paused. "Did you notice if they were wearing a gold necklace?"

"They were—it had a glowing red gem on it. I didn't see their face, though. Who was that?"

"I don't know... I didn't see their face either."

* * *

I stepped off the bus, following my classmates as they strode along the pathway toward the school. The morning sun hung low over the rooftops. Fallen leaves lay scattered across the school's front lawn, and a chill hung in the air.

"Sadie," I murmured to myself, rehearsing what I wanted to say, "remember how we cast a hex on Nerissa? Well—" I shook my head. "How am I supposed to even say this? Okay, okay. Sadie, I need to talk to you. A demon prince is—ugh! No, that's no good either! All right, Sadie, I—"

My thoughts were interrupted by a sneering laugh in the distance. It had come from the student parking lot. I peered toward it, my brows rising. Nerissa and Pauline stood by Sadie's black-and-red Mustang, looking into the open driver's side door. Pauline had something in her hand—a folded, black parasol. My eyes widened as I hurried toward the two girls.

Sadie was sitting in the driver's seat. She glanced warily at the sunlight on the pavement below before glaring up at Pauline. "I said give it back!"

"What, this?" The centaur snickered. She held out the parasol.

Sadie reached for it, but when her hand emerged into the morning sunlight, she yelped and snatched it back inside the car. She cradled her fingers. "Pauline, you jerk!"

The two other girls laughed. My tail lashed as I hurried across the parking lot. Sadie glowered at the bullies, baring her fangs with a hiss. She lunged out of the car, reaching for her stolen parasol. Pauline's hooves clopped across the asphalt as she backed away, holding the parasol out of Sadie's reach. Sadie clenched her teeth in pain. "Give that back!"

I noticed a smell like something burning. Wisps of smoke were rising from Sadie's exposed skin. "Hey!" I strode up to them. "Stop it, you're hurting her!"

A whoosh of air swirled around Sadie. She blinked in surprise, then lowered the hand she had been holding up against the sun. She peered down at the red tinged shadow falling across her face and arms, then up at my outstretched wing. "Lesley!"

Pauline rolled her eyes at me. "Wow, aren't you such a hero?" She tossed the parasol at my feet, and she and Nerissa headed away across the parking lot.

Sadie hugged me. "Thank you!"

"It seemed like the obvious thing to do."

She kept hugging me. "You're the best!" A moment later, she released me, looking embarrassed. "Sorry. I didn't mean to get all huggy on you like that."

I smiled. "It okay."

She took her parasol and unfurled it above her head. "You know what? You're just the kind of friend I need—by which I mean a friend with wings that can shade me from the sun." We both laughed.

We approached the school's front entrance. I remembered what I'd meant to tell her, and my smile faded.

"Sadie, remember that hex we cast on Nerissa a little while ago? There's something I need to tell you."

"Oh, that reminds me…" She stopped, glancing away. "So, um, I've been researching cambions a bit. I thought it might be interesting because there's so much I don't know about your kind. But I found out that, to cambions, magic is like a drug. It can be addictive." Sadie's expression was somber. "I guess it's a good thing we decided to stop using magic against Nerissa."

I chewed my lip. "Yeah, I guess it is."

"Wait, you found out, too? That's what you wanted to talk about, isn't it?"

Slowly, I nodded. I couldn't tell her anything now.

Sadie threw her arms around me again. "You have this amazing ability, but it's too dangerous to use. I can't imagine how disappointed you must feel."

I looked at her. "You have no idea."

13

The Summoning

My tail swayed listlessly as I hunched over my desk. The afternoon sun streamed in through my bedroom window, falling across my desk as I squinted at the pages of a textbook.

I was startled by a fluttering shadow that fell across the book. A soft tapping came from the windowpane. Perched on the sill outside, pecking at the glass, was a raven. It carried a folded paper in its beak.

I leaned forward over my desk to open the window. The raven flitted away for a second as I slid the pane upward. The bird landed on the sill again and hopped inside. It dropped the paper on my desk and cawed at me. Once I had taken the note in my hands, the raven spread its wings and flew back out through the window.

I glanced at my bedroom door, checking to see that it was closed, before unfolding the note. It was scrawled with spidery handwriting.

Come to my shop tonight at a quarter 'til eleven, and be ready for your first lesson.
—*Balthazar Crowley*

* * *

The cold night air rushed past me as I pedaled along the street. Some of the signs above the storefronts still glowed, but there was no traffic and the sidewalks were empty. I steered my bike down a sidestreet and coasted into the deeper darkness beneath the trees. Soon, I came to the warlock's shop.

I knocked on the door. "Hello?"

Balthazar peered out. "Come in, Lesley, come in."

Flickering candlelight filled the shop, illuminating the rows of bottles and jars on the shelves. Ginger stood on her driftwood perch, her beady eyes gazing down at me. The bird cawed as if saying hello. Balthazar directed me to sit at a small table in the middle of the room. Three items were arranged on the table—some dried flower petals, some chicken bones, and a blue tinged crystal.

Balthazar sat at the table across from me. He gestured at the objects. "Tell me, what do you feel coming from these?"

I thought back to the feeling in my mother's workshop and in the forest. I could feel it here too—that same sense of peace and calm. It was coming from the magical ingredients on the shelves around me. I concentrated, trying to focus on just the objects on the table. They exuded that same feeling, but it was hard to distinguish it from the sensations coming from the other items.

The longer I concentrated, the more it seemed different shades of emotion were coming off each of the items in the shop. Some jars on a nearby shelf emanated a sense of readiness and vigilance, while certain crystals felt cold and somber. I realized that even though the items on the table were all different, the sense I got from them was exactly the same. I opened my eyes. "They sort of feel... warm. Like settling into a hot bath or a cup of hot cocoa after being out in the cold."

Balthazar smiled. "Very good. In magical terminology, we would say that they all have the same essence. In this case, that warmth you describe is the essence of healing." He rose from his seat. "This way, please."

I followed him around the counter at the back. He led me through the back room and outside to a small lot behind the building. Above our heads, an electric lamp buzzed, filling the lot with a dull yellow glow. Another table stood in the middle of the lot, holding a collection of jars. Next to the table was a cast iron cauldron with a fire underneath. Steam rose from the bubbling water inside the cauldron.

Ginger glided down and perched on Balthazar's shoulder. The warlock led me across the lot's cracked pavement. I cleared my throat. "Can I ask something?"

"Of course."

"I thought magic came from the wellsprings. What are the ingredients for?"

"What comes from the wellsprings is raw magic. That stuff is wild and untamed, almost impossible to use directly. But when it seeps into things—minerals, plants, animals, even you and I—it imbues them with magical properties of their own. This secondary magic is what we harness with witchcraft."

We came to the table. I peered down at the dozen jars arranged along the tabletop. "Is that different from how, say… sorcery works?"

Balthazar raised an eyebrow. "Should I be concerned that you're asking about a form of black magic?"

"I'm just curious."

He sighed. "Witchcraft, along with most other schools of magic, uses power that originates from the wellsprings. But sorcery uses a different power, one from beyond this world. Furthermore, sorcery is all about following rules—about submitting to authority and rigidly observing rituals. Witchcraft, on the other hand, allows for creativity."

From the table, Balthazar took a jar of peppercorns and another filled with rock salt. "We'll start with something simple." He sprinkled a little of each jar's contents into the cauldron's bubbling water. "Fire burning pure and bright, send up sparks into the night."

The lamp above the shop's back door flickered and dimmed. With a pop, a glowing point of light leaped out of the water, rising like an ember from a campfire. The water fizzed as more embers popped out, drifting into the air. I gazed up at the column of sparks, smiling with delight.

The sparks drifted away, and the electric light came back on. "The words of the incantation don't have to be exact," Balthazar explained. "They are merely a tool to help you focus."

"Does it have to rhyme?"

"Rhyming is traditional, but not necessary." He handed me the jars. "Now, you give it a try."

I peered down at the boiling water and sprinkled some salt and pepper from the jars. "Fire burning pure and bright, send up sparks into the night."

I waited, but the only thing that rose from the water were bubbles and wisps of steam. I frowned. "Fire burning pure and bright," I repeated, "send up sparks into the night!"

Still nothing. I turned to Balthazar. "Why isn't it working?"

"It is not enough to merely say the words," the warlock explained. "You must focus the magic through them."

I drew in a breath, trying to find that sense of peace I remembered from the forest. I spoke the incantation again.

But again, nothing happened.

I shoved the jars back down on the table. "I'm the daughter of a witch and a demon. I thought that meant I was supposed to be good at magic!"

"You may have the talent," Balthazar said, "but there is talent, and then there is practice. You must be patient."

* * *

A few days later, my mom was kneeling in the back yard by one of the empty garden plots. It looked like she'd been busy finishing them. She'd put in trim along the edges, and the soil was tilled and ready for planting. She removed a glove, tossing it aside before wiping her eye. Was she crying?

I stepped onto the patio. "Mom, what's wrong?"

She looked up at me. "Word got out that I'm the witch who ran away with an incubus. My boss thought I was scaring away customers, so..."

My stomach sank. "Oh no! Did you lose your job? I'm so sorry. This is my fault! I shouldn't have come to the store."

She got up and gave me a hug. "It's not your fault, sweetie. I'll start looking for another job first thing tomorrow. Just be aware that money might get a little tight soon." She tried giving me a smile. "But don't worry. We'll get through this."

I wandered back inside, a knot in the pit of my stomach. Despite what my mom had said, it *was* my fault she'd lost her job. If not for my stupid wings and devil horns, she'd still be happily working at the flower shop.

I stepped into my bedroom, chewing my lip as I glanced at the dresser. I quietly closed the door behind me before opening the dresser's bottom drawer, where I'd hidden my jewelry box. Inside, the amulet's gold chain glistened, the red gemstone glowing softly. Next to it was the tattered summoning scroll. Also hidden in the drawer were some candles, a book of matches, and a small, crudely carved wooden idol. I'd stashed them there days ago, but so far I'd chickened out on what I was planning to do. But if my mom had lost her job because of me...

I stuffed the necklace and the other items into my jacket pockets, squared my shoulders, and headed out into the brisk evening air. I paced quickly along the sidewalk—I had to get away before my mom realized because I didn't want Rugby along for what I was about to do. I turned a corner into the woods. Dead leaves crunched under my feet. Through the trees ahead stood the solitary stone chimney. I stepped into the clearing.

"Hello?" I called. "Anyone here?" When it seemed I was alone, I pulled the amulet from my pocket. I held up the golden chain, watching the jewel sway in the wind. I bit my lip and clasped the chain around my neck. Calm instantly washed over me, stilling my swishing tail.

I unrolled the scroll and peered at the angular text. I grabbed a stick from under one of the trees and kicked away the leaves from a patch of dirt. I dragged the stick across the ground, tracing out a circle, and filled the circle with runes and angular shapes matching the diagram on the scroll. Finally, I placed seven candles around the circle and lit them one by one. Even with the clarity that enveloped me, my heart thumped uneasily. I drew in a breath and read the incantation.

As soon as I finished, fire burst up from within the summoning circle. The flames swirled, forming a column that reached as high as the treetops. Hot wind gusted through the clearing, carrying the stench of rotten eggs. A shadowy shape appeared within the pillar of fire, quickly resolving into the form of a man.

The fire went out. The hot wind rushed back into the portal, blowing out the candles and knocking them over. I blinked at the man who stood in the middle of the charred patch of earth. He was tall, with messy bangs draped over his brow and stubble covering his square jaw. I didn't know why, but somehow he seemed familiar.

He smiled warmly. "Lesley, it's so good to finally meet you."

I shivered. "Who are you?"

"It's me, Lesley. It's your father, Caelum."

My eyes went wide. "You're... you're my father? Asmodeus sent *you*?"

"*I* requested that he send me. I would have begged him if I had to." He stepped forward, spreading his arms invitingly.

"Stay back!" I pulled the wooden idol from my pocket, holding it up to ward him off.

Caelum blinked at the crude charm. "What's this about? Haven't you summoned me because you want to learn sorcery?"

"This charm gives me power over you, demon! I command you to teach me how to shapeshift into human form!"

He crooked an eyebrow, then closed his hand over the idol. "This hasn't been enchanted properly," he said, taking it from me. "Even then, it's the wrong kind for an incubus." He tossed the idol over his shoulder. "Is that what you think I am? Just some evil demon?"

It's a trick. He's trying to manipulate me.

"Lesley," Caelum continued, "you're in no danger from me. You're my daughter." He reached out to take my hand.

I backed away. "Don't touch me!"

He didn't flinch at my words but kept watching me with gentle concern. "Come with me to the Scholomance. I'm sure you'll fit in there much better than you do in Misty Hollow."

"No. I just want to appear human again, nothing else. Please!"

He shook his head sadly. "I'm sorry. I want to help you, but I am bound by my contract with Asmodeus. I cannot act against his wishes. Come with me. Pledge yourself to my master, and I will teach you the power of shapeshifting."

"And become Asmodeus's minion, like you? No thanks."

Caelum nodded solemnly. "If that is your wish." He turned, trudging away across the clearing. "But if you change your mind, or if you need anything from me, come find me here." He smiled back over his shoulder. There was a puff of smoke and flame, and he was gone.

I stared blankly at the spot he had been standing. A moment later, I frowned down at the amulet around my neck. I tore off the necklace and crumpled up the scroll, clutching them in my trembling fist. I was about to fling them into the underbrush, but I hesitated.

The amulet's calm brushed across my skin like the warmth of a candle. I watched the gold chain glitter in the fading twilight, watched the red jewel as it glowed so softly, pulsing with the rhythm of my heart.

* * *

I stood by my locker, my classmates shuffling by as I stared blankly at the wall. A moment later, I slammed my locker shut. Around me, the hallway quieted a bit. I glanced around, glaring at one of the students who was looking at me. With a huff, I hurried away along the hall.

My ears twitched as the sound of hooves came clicking toward me. "Hey Lesley," a voice sneered.

"You *really* don't want to mess with me right now, Murk."

"I heard how you helped Sadie by shading her from the sun." Murk stepped in front of me, blocking my path. He pressed his hands together as if in prayer. "You're such an *angel*. Oh, wait, I forgot—you're the opposite of that."

I ground my teeth. "Shut up, Murk!" I shoved my way past him.

"Oh, I'm sorry." The satyr chuckled. "I didn't mean to *demonize* you!"

I squeezed my fists tighter. "I said shut up!" Without thinking, I whispered a magic word. "*Impulsio!*"

Murk lurched back, slamming into the lockers behind him. He winced, rubbing his shoulder before looking at me with wide eyes. My brows climbed, and I hurried away. I headed into the cafeteria, brushing past the other students, but I slowed. A smile spread across my face. "Well, that certainly shut him up," I said, chuckling to myself.

"What's so funny?" Sadie asked from behind me.

I almost jumped. "Uh, nothing." I adjusted the collar of my shirt, hoping she hadn't seen the gold chain around my neck.

14

The Scholomance

With a yawn, I stepped into my bedroom. I rubbed my tired eyes, unslung my satchel, and set it on my desk. I tugged the amulet out from under my shirt collar and pulled open my dresser's bottom drawer. I opened the jewelry box but hesitated. The necklace's calming presence brushed against my skin, inviting me to let it seep into me.

No. I reached up to unlatch the chain, but footsteps were coming down the hall. I stuffed the necklace back into my shirt.

"Lesley," my mother called. She peeked through my bedroom door. "Sadie is here for music practice." She tilted her head. "You looking for something?"

I glanced down at the open dresser drawer and pulled out a paperback book at random. "Uh, yeah, but I found it."

"*The Great Gatsby*?" my mother asked. "I thought you hated that book."

"Um, I might try reading it again." I stood, kicked the drawer closed, and set the book atop the dresser. "You said Sadie's here?" My mother nodded. I grabbed my guitar and headed to the living room.

"Hi, Lesley." Sadie smiled as I entered. She stood in front of a music stand with a printout of the lyrics. I sat down and set my guitar on my knee. Sadie looked at me. "You okay?"

"I'm just a bit tired. I… had some trouble sleeping last night is all." I obviously wasn't going to mention last night's illicit magic lesson with Balthazar. I grabbed my guitar pick and pressed my fingers to the strings.

Sadie began to sing, and I plucked notes in time with her. Soon, though, I lost the timing. "Sorry," I muttered. "I had this figured out last time."

Sadie regarded me. "It's okay if you don't want to practice today."

The calm feeling from the jewel above my heart seemed to nudge me, offering to help. *No,* I told it. But then I looked at Sadie. *Fine, just this once.* I took a breath, drawing in the clarity the amulet offered me, allowing it to wash away my fatigue. "No, really, I'm fine," I told Sadie. "Let's keep going."

* * *

I peered at the row of jars arranged on the table in front of me. Next to me, the cauldron bubbled, wisps of vapor rising into the cold night air. I looked up at Balthazar. He stood on the other side of the table, watching me with a carefully neutral expression. His familiar spirit, the raven Ginger, was perched on his shoulder.

I scrunched my brow, hesitating. I reached for a jar of dried rose petals and glanced at Balthazar. His expression gave away nothing. I bit my lip, my hand hovering over the jars. "An aroma sweet and comforting," I said, recalling the spell I was supposed to cast. My hand landed on a jar filled with chunks of honeycomb. I looked up at the warlock again, but his face remained unreadable.

I opened the jar and pulled out a piece of sticky beeswax, then dropped the honeycomb into the cauldron. I spread my hands above the bubbling water. "May the sweetness of this honey bring an aroma sweet and comforting."

I jumped back as seething froth hissed up from the cauldron. A puff of stinking black smoke erupted, billowing like a mushroom cloud. I coughed, waving my hand in front of my face.

"You should have added the rose petals," said Balthazar. "The first line of your spell should have been 'may the sweet scent of these roses bring,' which would have reminded you of this fact."

I gave the cauldron a kick, making it ring like a gong. "I *still* can't get anything to work! I can't even remember a basic incantation."

Balthazar stepped around the table. "Why are you impatient with this?"

"Because—" I hesitated. "Because, you know, I'm part demon, which makes me hot-headed and stuff."

He raised an eyebrow at me. "I've been around long enough to know the stereotypes about the fae aren't true. Really, why are you in such a rush to learn witchcraft?"

I swallowed. "Because I'm afraid I won't be able to do it. I have a warlock friend at school who was never able to go beyond basic spells. What if I can't either? What will I do then?"

* * *

Above my head, skeletal branches rattled in the cold breeze. Through the trees, the setting sun seemed poised on a distant hilltop. I'd messaged Zack earlier, asking if he wanted to go for a walk in the woods, but he'd said he was busy. I went for a walk anyway, alone except for Rugby trotting at my side.

"You don't think Zack is avoiding me, do you?" I asked the dog.

Rugby peered up at me, his tongue lolling as he panted.

"Don't give me that. I know you're smarter than you look."

He whimpered.

I shook my head. "Why am I talking to a *dog* about my problems?"

A few minutes later, a fiery glow appeared between the trees. At first I thought it was the sunset, but I realized it was coming from the wrong direction and that the sun had already set. I slowed my pace, creeping cautiously along a muddy path. A breeze stirred, sending fallen leaves skittering across the ground. As I drew closer to the strange, fiery glow, the wind warmed, and I caught a whiff of rotten eggs.

I peeked between two trees, and my eyes went wide. On the ground, in the middle of a small clearing, was what looked like a pool of fire. The flames boiled and bubbled, sending swirls into the air. Seven candles surrounded the pool, and in front of it stood a black-cloaked figure.

Rugby backed away, tugging at the leash. I stayed put, my eyes fixed on the flaming portal. I gasped as another dark shape appeared, this time within the fiery pool. The silhouette seemed to have two heads atop a single set of broad shoulders. Two pairs of burning eyes peered out as the dark shape rose up.

Thankfully, the monster seemed to be struggling to emerge. It reached out, clawing at the earth around the pool with huge paws. Then the ground shook. The creature gave a rumbling growl, trying to hold on, but was sucked back down. The fire sputtered and went out, leaving only a charred patch on the forest floor.

The warm wind died down. The cloaked figure hung their head in disappointment. They took up a book from the ground and flipped through its yellowed pages.

I was trembling. I took a step back, but some fallen leaves crunched under my foot. The figure spun toward me. I couldn't see a face within the shadows of the hood, but I did see a glowing crimson jewel. I screamed and turned to run.

* * *

The next morning, I crept out of the house before my mother could ask where I was going, heading into the woods. Frost clung to the leaves, gleaming in the sunlight that slanted in between the boughs. I stood in the shadow of the old stone chimney. The amulet was clasped around my neck, and I held out the crumpled scroll, peering at the spell I'd used to summon Caelum. Surely, some of the magic words would do something on their own. Maybe some would be useful—something I could use to protect myself. "*Inferis!*" I incanted.

Nothing happened.

I looked at the next word. "*Porta!*"

Still nothing.

I picked another word at random. "*Precatio!*"

Useless.

"Oh, come on!" I shouted, resisting the urge to crumple the scroll again. I sank back against the chimney, dropping the scroll and hiding my face in my hands.

Footsteps crunched across the leaves. I looked up to find Caelum watching me.

"What's the matter?"

I sniffed and wiped at my face. "Why should you care?"

"Because you're my daughter."

I frowned at him. "If you really care, then help me. Someone is trying to use sorcery against me. I need a way to defend myself. Or better yet, I need to go back to the human world, which I can't do without shapeshifting."

He shook his head sadly. "My contract won't allow me to help you directly." Caelum paused and offered me his hand. "Come, let me take you to visit the Scholomance. If you are to choose between going there and staying in Misty Hollow, it's only fair you see both options."

"No, I'm not—" I blinked. *They'll have spellbooks at the Scholomance. Maybe I can steal one.* "I mean, um, this isn't some sort of trick? You're not just trying to kidnap me, are you?"

"If Asmodeus could have simply kidnapped you, he would have already. No, the only way you'll join us is by your own free will."

I drew in a breath. "In that case, yes, I would like to see this Scholomance place... but just a quick visit. I'm not agreeing to go there."

He laughed. "I'm glad you're suspicious. That's good. Now come with me. Just for a quick visit."

I followed Caelum into the woods, past the point the dryad had warned me not to cross. We were in the Sacred Grove, where distance no longer worked the same. I wondered where exactly the Scholomance was—it could be anywhere in the world, I supposed, because the ever-shifting paths could take us anywhere.

My tail twitched, and my wings refused to stay folded against my back. I hung back a short distance, studying the man who claimed to be my father. Maybe he wasn't really, for all I knew. Maybe he was only saying that to manipulate me, to gain my trust. But he was showing me such kindness and gentleness, and I wanted to trust him. I shook my head, trying to chase away the feeling.

After a few minutes of hiking, I cleared my throat. "So how far is it?"

"Not far. The trick is avoiding the dryads. They don't like it when demons come here." His brow furrowed, and he ducked into the underbrush along the side of the path, motioning for me to do the same. "Someone is coming," he whispered.

I crouched next to him. A woman in a park ranger uniform strode quickly along the path. After she passed, Caelum smirked at me. "I believe the humans have an expression—'speak of the devil, and he shall appear.'" I raised an eyebrow at him. He chuckled and stepped back onto the path.

The trail continued through the forest, over roots and fallen logs and around mossy boulders. At one point, I smelled salt spray in the air and swore I could hear the ocean. After that, I noticed a change in the light streaming between the branches. The sun was much higher than it had been. The further we went, the further the sun climbed, until it shone from directly above. The path wound uphill, and my ears popped as the air pressure changed. The sky grew overcast, and fog drifted among the trees.

We emerged from the forest. I looked down at a small lake nestled in an alpine valley. The tops of the mountains were shrouded in mist and clouds, while their lower slopes were covered in bristly pine trees. A stream cascaded along the narrow valley, plunging into the lake. An old, mossy stone bridge crossed over the churning water, and on the far side stood the ruins of a castle. Even though it was midday, the storm clouds overhead shrouded the castle and the valley in shadow.

I leaned against a tree to catch my breath—the thin mountain air was making me dizzy. "Where are we?"

"Romania," Caelum answered. "In the part of the country once known as 'Transylvania.'" He led me down the rocky slope and across the bridge over the stream that flowed into the lake. I stepped carefully across the mossy stones, peering down at the inky waters. A splash in the distance made me shudder. Out of the corner of my eye, I glimpsed something rise from beneath the surface. It was slimy and sinuous, perhaps a neck or tentacle, but before I could get a better look, it slipped beneath the water again, leaving only a circle of spreading ripples.

Thunder rumbled as we approached the castle. Caelum led me through the front gate into a small courtyard. He performed a spell to unlock a weathered wooden door at the base of a ruined tower. The air inside was musty and stale, and the small chamber was dark. Caelum held a glimmering flame above his open palm as he led me down a spiral staircase. I brushed past tangles of cobwebs, getting some caught on my horns and wing-claws.

Ahead of me, Caelum was nothing more than a dark shape silhouetted by the flame in his hand. Despite my rapidly growing uneasiness, I kept following him down the staircase, further and further into the earth. With each step I took, the more oppressive the darkness became. I don't know how long it was before we finally came to a landing, but we stood before another wooden door flanked by torches. The torchlight seemed smothered by the darkness, the glow pooling around the door and going no further.

Caelum knocked, and the door creaked inward. I followed him into a long, pillared hall, my footsteps echoing from the stone walls. The vast hall was lit by more torches, as well as a row of grotesque chandeliers hanging on iron chains from the vaulted ceiling. Like the torches outside, their light didn't seem to reach far, leaving pitch black shadows in corners and alcoves.

A pair of guards stood in front of us. They were dressed in medieval-looking armor—iron helmets and vests of chain mail—and each carried a wicked-looking pike. They crossed their pikes in front of us, barring our path.

"Who goes there?" one of the guards asked in a rasping voice.

Caelum smiled warmly. "Jasper, is that you under that helmet? How are the wife and kids?"

The guard removed his helmet. His skin was greenish, and he had an elongated nose and ears. He was a goblin. The guard gave Caelum an impatient glare. "State your business here, incubus."

The warmth in Caelum's expression faded, but he maintained a polite expression. "I'm here on official business for Prince Asmodeus. The details don't concern you."

The green-skinned man glanced at me, sniffing the air. "Well now—a half-blood." He looked at Caelum suspiciously. "What are you bringing her here for?"

"I told you, the details of my assignment are not your concern."

The goblin grumbled to himself. "Papers?"

"Come, now, Jasper, it's me—" The goblin swung his pike down, pointing it at Caelum's chest. Caelum just seemed annoyed, though. "Very well." He reached as if to pluck something out of the air, and a tattered parchment appeared in a puff of smoke. He held it up for the guard to see. Finally, the goblin lowered his pike, although his suspicious look didn't change. The guard gave me the evil eye as I followed Caelum.

I peered through one of the doorways between the pillars along the hall. A group of half a dozen people in black robes were gathered around a rune-filled circle drawn in chalk on the floor. Many of them looked like they were my age—they must be students. A wizened old man with a long, white beard peered down at the circle, clutching a staff in his gnarled hands as he recited an incantation.

Most of the other rooms seemed empty. "This school doesn't seem to have very many students," I said.

"Only ten students are admitted each year," Caelum explained. "Only the best are allowed to attend. But don't worry, your admission to the Scholomance is guaranteed."

"Why? Because Asmodeus commanded it?"

"No, because you *are* one of the best. Asmodeus is sure of it, and so am I."

We entered another room along the hallway. It was a library. Bookshelves lined the walls along both sides, and rows of shelves stood further to the back. Iron chandeliers hung from the vaulted ceiling, and chairs and tables were arranged around a fire pit in the center of the room. A few black-robed students sat here and there, leafing through the pages of the books.

I followed Caelum over to a girl at one of the tables. The plain black robe she wore was a complete mismatch for her striking looks, which I'll admit I was immediately jealous of. Auburn hair flowed down to her shoulders, and her brilliant green eyes gave a sense of mystery and danger. When she saw Caelum approaching, a smile split her face. She hopped up and ran over to give him a hug. "Uncle Cael!"

"It's wonderful to see you again," Caelum said with a smile. He turned to me. "Lesley, this is my niece, Carina. Carina, allow me to introduce you to my daughter, Lesley."

"You finally found her?" Carina shook my hand vigorously. "Caelum told me he's been looking for you. I'm so glad he found you. Will you be joining us at the Scholomance next year?"

"I'm... thinking about it," I lied. "Um, are you a cambion like me?"

"No, I'm a full-blooded succubus." She tossed her head, sending silky hair cascading. "You couldn't even tell, could you? My disguise is just about perfect, isn't it?"

"Disguise? Wow, yeah, I'd say it's perfect." I paused for a moment. "Uh, by 'disguise,' you mean you're using a shapeshifting spell?"

"Yeah, obviously." She pointed to her forehead. "Do you see any horns right now?"

"So," I asked carefully, "is it hard to learn shapeshifting?"

She shrugged. "It wasn't hard for me. I'm sure it'll be easy for you, too."

"I see. Um, to shapeshift, do you have to, like, speak an incantation, or..."

Carina raised an eyebrow. I glanced over to see Caelum shooting her a warning look.

"You're sly," he said to me, without malice. "That's good. You'll need that here. But I'm afraid you won't be getting any clues about the shapeshifting spell from us."

Carina gave me a wry smile. "I like her already," she said to Caelum.

"So tell me," he said to her, "how is my brother doing? I've been away so long."

It was strange listening to them talk about normal things, like family life or how school was going. I could almost forget they were actually demons in disguise and we were in a dungeon of a library at a school that taught the black art of sorcery.

After a minute or so, I glanced toward the bookshelves. "While you guys talk, mind if I look around?"

"Go right ahead," Caelum said to me, continuing his conversation with his niece.

My tail swished nervously as I headed for the bookshelves. I scanned over the books, now and then casting a wary glance at Caelum and Carina. A lot of their titles were in languages I didn't know, but enough were in English that I was able to find my way around. One book in particular caught my attention. It was bound in worn, red-dyed leather. Its title, written in gold ink that was beginning to flake off, said *Spells and Magic of Incubi and Succubi.* My heart thumped. I cast another glance over my shoulder. Quickly, I unzipped my satchel and reached for the book.

A greenish hand closed around my wrist. I yelped, turning to face the goblin guard from the front gate. "You little thief!" he rasped. He dragged me toward the library entrance. "You're coming with me!"

I struggled against his grip. "Caelum!"

There was a puff of smoke, and Caelum was suddenly face to face with the goblin. "Jasper!" he hissed. "Let go of my daughter."

"But she's a thief! She tried to steal a book!"

Caelum continued to glare at the guard. "I gave you an order. Do I need to report your disobedience to Asmodeus?"

The goblin paled. A moment later, he let go of my wrist. "Little thief," he muttered as he stepped past me.

"I want to go home," I said to Caelum, my voice quaking. "Take me home now!"

* * *

Sighing with relief, I strode into the clearing with the old stone chimney. "I'm sorry about Jasper," said Caelum, stepping up behind me. "He gets paranoid like that. If you like, I can put in a word with Asmodeus and have him… removed from his post. Please don't let him dissuade you from attending the Scholomance."

"I'm not going to that stupid school." I trudged off across the clearing.

In a flicker of flame, Caelum appeared in front of me. "Please, Lesley. You'd be so much happier there. Surely you can see that."

"I don't think so. Now get out of my way."

He regarded me for a long moment before stepping aside. "Very well. But I'll still be here if you change your mind."

I stepped past him, chewing my lip—I had an idea, but wasn't sure if it would work. Once a bit of distance separated me and Caelum, I drew in a breath, turned, and spread my palm. "*Ignis!*" A burst of crimson fire shot from my hand.

Caelum's eyes widened, and he lifted his hands. "*Praesidium!*" he cried. A circle of scintillating red energy appeared in the air in front of him, countless miniature lightning bolts dancing across its glassy surface. The magical shield deflected the fire before vanishing.

I was just as surprised as him. Quickly, I spread my palms outward like he had. "*Praesidium!*" A wave of the same glassy, crimson energy spread out in front of me. I gasped, smiling with delight. "Oh my god, I can't believe that actually worked!"

Caelum wrinkled his nose at me. "Well, aren't you clever? Go ahead and gloat, but don't think you'll be able to trick me into revealing another spell like that." He stalked back toward the forest but glanced at me, a faint smile on his lips. "You are so much like your mother." He vanished in a puff of smoke.

15

Dabbling with Magic

I looked out from the stage across the school auditorium. Students and parents filled the rows of seats, watching as Sadie and I performed our song for the talent show. Sadie stood next to me, singing into a microphone, while I plucked notes on my guitar.

Sadie was definitely having fun. She danced and swayed dramatically, reaching out an imploring hand toward the audience as she sang. I sat with my wings half-spread and my tail curled to the side because Sadie had insisted it would look cool, and I agreed it did.

Something tugged against my hand, and I dropped my guitar pick. Sadie stopped singing, and silence fell over the auditorium. "Hold on... technical difficulties," Sadie said into the microphone as I scrambled to grab the pick from the floor. I strummed the strings, and Sadie smoothly resumed the song. For the rest of our performance, I had to concentrate to keep my tail from twitching.

Sadie drew the microphone close, drawing out the song's final words as the last note from my guitar rang out. The two of us stepped forward as the audience applauded. I took a bow but was too late to notice Sadie had curtsied instead. A few chuckles rose from the audience. Sadie crooked an eyebrow at me but smiled. "Good job," she murmured as we stepped down from the stage.

We returned to our seats. "Nice job, Lesley," said Zack.

I sat between him and Sadie, setting my guitar down between my knees. "Even though I screwed up there in the middle?"

I tried not to blush as he placed a reassuring hand on mine. "You got back on track just fine."

The curtains were drawn closed, and Principal Constance stepped onto the stage. "Next up," she said into the microphone, "is Nerissa Howard, who will be performing to the music of Dance of the Sugar Plum Fairy."

The principal stepped off the stage as the auditorium lights dimmed. The curtains opened, and a spotlight focused on Nerissa. She was wearing a frilly ballet dress covered in sparkling sequins. She sauntered out onto the stage and curtsied, eliciting some claps from the audience and a whistle or two from the boys. Music played, and Nerissa spread her arms, twirling as she tiptoed across the stage. She kicked her legs in the air as she skipped from one side of the stage to the other, eliciting more cheers.

"Wow, she's actually pretty good," Zack murmured.

I jabbed him in the side with an elbow. "Hey, whose side are you on?"

He shrugged. "I'm just saying…"

I wrinkled my nose as Nerissa continued to skip and twirl. My flub on stage hadn't been an accident—the invisible tug on my arm had been a spell, and I'd have bet anything Nerissa had cast it.

The amulet around my neck offered me a sense of steely calm. *I could do the same to her.*

No, I told myself.

But she'd already done far worse. What's wrong with a little payback?

I was almost startled—that wasn't *my* thought, was it? I fingered the gold chain around my neck. It almost seemed like the amulet was whispering things to me. Then something else whispered into my mind—a magic word. It was a curse, I somehow knew, one that would inflict pain. *No!* I thought, horrified.

But the amulet had stopped whispering. Or had I only been imagining it had? Had those actually been *my* inner thoughts? I concentrated on the amulet, trying to listen, but no more whispers came from it. I probably had just been imagining things. The magic word that had come into my head was most likely gibberish.

More applause rose from the audience as Nerissa spun gracefully. I narrowed my eyes—I didn't want to hurt her, but I was still mad at her. She'd made me fumble during my performance. It would only be fair if I did the same thing to her, right? I drew in a slow breath, inviting the amulet's cold clarity into me, letting it flow into my heart. I focused my gaze on Nerissa's feet. "*Impulsio.*"

Her foot slipped out from under her, and she thudded to her hands and knees. A gasp rose from the audience. Nerissa scrambled back up, glancing at the floor in confusion. She peered out at the audience, cheeks red with embarrassment. I held my face still, trying not to smirk.

Sadie turned to me. "Did you say something?"

* * *

Through my bedroom window, gray clouds blanketed the sky. A cold wind whistled through the crack under my windowpane. I set my satchel on my desk and hung my jacket across the back of my chair. I tugged the chain of my necklace out from under my shirt collar, letting it hang in front of my chest as I looked in the mirror. The red jewel shone, dimming and brightening in time with my heartbeat.

I almost jumped as footsteps clomped along the hallway outside my door. I tore off the necklace, threw it in the bottom drawer of my dresser, and kicked the drawer shut. I grabbed *The Great Gatsby* and reclined on my bed, pretending to read.

My mother burst through the door. "I just got off the phone with the principal. Apparently a boy named Mercury and the girl from the talent show, Nerissa, both accused you of using telekinesis on them." I looked up from my book, flinching when I saw the angry look in her eyes. "Lesley," she asked, "have you been dabbling with magic?"

I swallowed. Briefly, my eyes darted toward my dresser's bottom drawer. I sat up, opened my mouth, but hesitated.

"Did you speak with Asmodeus?" my mother pressed. "Did he give you something that would let you cast spells?"

My insides squirmed. Then the knot in my stomach vanished as I narrowed my eyes. "Yes, in fact, I *did* speak to Asmodeus," I growled. "He told me I could learn to do magic... which was more than *you* ever did for me!"

My mother's eyes widened. She opened her mouth but closed it again. Finally, she turned and stomped back out to the hallway, slamming the door behind her.

* * *

Vapors bubbled from the cauldron, rising toward the starry sky. I held a jar of peppercorns in one hand and a jar of rock salt in the other. I sprinkled a little of each into the bubbling water and set them aside. I took a breath, drawing in the chill air, and spread my palms above the cauldron. "Fire burning pure and bright, send up sparks into the night."

The cauldron hissed and boiled. The light from the lamp above the door briefly flickered, and a glittering spark popped out of the bubbling water, rising into the air like a firefly. I waited. "That's it?" I said when no more sparks emerged. I clenched my fists. "Why is this still not working?"

Ginger, perched on the edge of the shop's roof, cawed. Balthazar sighed. "Lesley," he said carefully, "it may be that you lack sufficient aptitude with witchcraft in the same way your friend Zack does."

"But I can *sense* magic."

"Sensing magic is one thing. Manipulating it using these techniques is another."

But there are other techniques. Like sorcery. My stomach sank. "I'll never be able to learn shapeshifting, will I?"

Balthazar rubbed his temples. "I understand your desire to appear human again. Your transformation must have been traumatic. But... it's possible shapeshifting is beyond your abilities."

"Then what am I supposed to do?"

He leaned down to look me in the eye. "My advice would be to try and accept yourself as you are."

With a fluttering of feathers, Ginger swooped down from the roof, cawing as she dove toward the narrow alley next to Balthazar's shop. A pale, porcelain face was peeking out from the shadows. My eyes widened.

The startled vampire spun, hurrying away into the darkness. "Wait!" I called after her. "Sadie!" I dashed through the alley and out onto the sidewalk, only in time to hear an engine rev. I watched as Sadie's black and red Mustang peeled away into the night.

* * *

I peered out through the school bus window at the dim, gray morning. Specks of snow were drifting down from the sky. The bus stopped in front of the school, and my classmates, wrapped in their winter coats, disembarked. A chill crept through me. I had no idea what to say to Sadie. Finally, I shuffled along the aisle and emerged onto the sidewalk.

The lawn in front of the school was brown and faded. The trees in front of the building were bare of leaves, the cold wind hissing through their branches. The engines of the buses rumbled, clouds of vapor billowing from their tail pipes as my classmates plodded toward the school. I stopped when I saw Sadie standing by the front steps, waiting. She was craning her neck, peering out at the crowd. A second later, she saw me and waved for me to come over. It wasn't a friendly sort of wave, but an urgent one.

I hesitated before stepping over to her. I couldn't look her in the eye. Wordlessly, Sadie ushered me a little way onto the lawn, away from the other students. She stopped beneath one of the leafless trees. "I-I saw you last night behind the warlock's shop, casting some sort of spell."

Finally, I looked up at her. "You followed me, didn't you?" My voice sounded harsher than I had meant.

"I'm sorry. I know I probably shouldn't have. But rumors have been going around the school. Murk thought you shoved him with telekinesis, but he didn't tell anyone at first. But then there was the thing with Nerissa at the talent show. I thought I heard you say some kind of magic word. I was worried, and..." She swallowed, and I almost flinched at the hurt in her voice. "I thought we were friends. Why didn't you tell me?"

"I couldn't risk anyone finding out." I hesitated and tugged down the collar of my coat, revealing the gold chain around my neck. "This amulet lets me do sorcery. A demon prince gave it to me. He said he could teach me more, but that I would have to become his servant. I was hoping witchcraft could be a different way for me to do magic, but..." I chewed my lip, too afraid to explain the rest. "Look, Sadie, you can't tell *anyone*, okay?"

"Of course. You can trust me. You know that, right?" Sadie leaned in closer, lowering her voice. "And like, holy crap, you can do magic! That's awesome! But... I thought we decided it was too dangerous."

Anger welled up inside me. "No, *we* didn't decide that. *You* did."

"I'm only trying to help."

"I don't want your help!" I snapped.

Her fangs gleamed. "Fine." Sadie turned away.

I took a breath, my anger subsiding. "Sadie..."

But she was already hurrying past the other students as they went up the front steps. "Sadie, wait!" She disappeared inside, not looking back at me. For a long moment, I stood there in silence. Stinging feelings swirled through me as the cold wind blew past, until I couldn't tell the difference between the two anymore.

* * *

That afternoon, my wings drooped as I trudged away from the bus stop. Gray clouds covered the sky, and a blanket of newly fallen snow was spread across the lawns and rooftops. The cold wind sent snowflakes swirling across the ground. I hugged myself, fighting down a chill—one not just from the wintry weather. *I should have told her sooner.* I had hoped for a chance to apologize, but Sadie hadn't sat at our usual lunch table, and it hadn't looked like I was welcome at her new one.

My thoughts were interrupted by the thump of hooves approaching from behind. I turned to see Pauline cantering along the sidewalk, with Daphne skimming above the snow beside her, gossamer wings buzzing. Pauline thumped past me and spun, facing me as she came to a stop. Her horse tail swished angrily behind her. The centaur took out her phone, tapped on the screen, and held the device up. "You used magic on Nerissa at the talent show. Admit it!"

Daphne alighted next to her. She leveled a wand at me, holding it in a white-knuckled grip. "I've placed protective wards, so you can't hurt us. We're not afraid of you!"

The look on Daphne's face suggested otherwise. I glanced at Pauline's phone. "Are you recording this or something?"

"Yes," Pauline growled. "Now admit what you did."

"And… and don't try anything!" Daphne stammered.

Pauline's hooves clicked as she came closer, holding her phone up to my face. "It's time to come clean, Lesley."

I scowled at her. "Get out of my way!" Without thinking, I squared my stance and thrust my hands forward, palms open. "*Praesidium!*"

A shock wave of crackling red energy burst out from my hands with a sound like thunder. Pauline yelped, staggering and dropping her phone as the wave of scarlet energy crashed over her. Daphne reeled backward, plopping down onto the snow. Her wings fluttered as she scrambled to her feet again. She looked at me, her eyes wide in fright.

I turned and ran. My wings unfurled instinctively, clawing at the air, itching to take flight.

16

Video Evidence

"It's time to come clean, Lesley," Pauline's voice came from the laptop speaker.

"Get out of my way!" The loudness of my own voice caused the speaker to rattle. The girl in the recording thrust her hands forward. There was a garbled sound that might have been a magic word, and a burst of energy erupted from her palm. The sound briefly cut out as static filled the screen. Next came a whirling view of the neighborhood, followed by a thunk and a shot of the overcast sky through out-of-focus flecks of snow. Fingers closed over part of the view, and the view swept across the neighbors' houses, finally showing me running away down the sidewalk, my wings and tail in full view. "Oh my god..." Pauline said.

The playback stopped, and the laptop screen went dark. Principal Constance turned the laptop toward herself and closed the lid. She peered at me from behind her desk with a disappointed gaze. My mother sat in the chair next to me, her arms folded across her chest.

"You used magic." My mother looked me in the eyes. "Lesley, why?"

"I got angry at them. I didn't mean to."

"No. Why did you go against my wishes and try to learn magic?"

"It was because of Nerissa. She's been using magic against me. And it gets worse—I saw a black-robed figure in the woods trying to open a portal to Hell!"

The principal shook her head. "I doubt very much that Nerissa would dabble in magic. And do you really expect me to believe some fanciful tale of a dark figure in the woods?"

"But—"

"I don't care what you think your reasons were for dabbling," my mother said. "How did you learn magic?"

I shivered at the anger that seethed beneath her words. "I hired a warlock to teach me."

"Who?"

"Balthazar Crowley."

Her brows rose. "Balthazar? But how did you pay for..." Her brows rose. "You traded him samples of your blood, didn't you?"

Slowly, I nodded.

She narrowed her eyes at me. "You are not to go see him ever again, understood?"

I swallowed. "Yes, Mother."

Principal Constance leaned forward in her chair. "Jane, it seems your daughter has shown herself to be a potential danger to the school. I'm giving her a three-day suspension."

My eyes widened. "But what about Nerissa?"

"During that time," the principal continued, ignoring me, "I'm sure you will discipline Lesley in whatever way you deem most appropriate."

The principal dismissed us. My mother took my hand, all but dragging me along as we marched down the empty hallway. When we reached the front entrance, she kept a

161

tight grip on my hand, like she thought I might try to escape. A cold wind swirled as ragged clouds raced by overhead.

She slammed the car door and kept her gaze fixed ahead as she drove us home. After several minutes of brooding silence, she finally spoke. "Why did you lie to me?" she asked, her tone dangerously quiet.

"You lied to me first!" I snapped. "You told me I couldn't do magic."

She turned to me, and I flinched at the flash of witch-fire in her eyes.

We pulled into the driveway, and my mom took my hand again. She dragged me into the foyer and down the hall to my bedroom. My eyes widened. "Mom, wait!"

"That wasn't witchcraft you used on those girls," my mother seethed. "You think I didn't recognize that spell? That was sorcery!" Her gaze darted around the room. She peered into my closet, then looked under my bed. Finally, her gaze fell on my dresser.

"Mom, no!" I pleaded.

One by one, she pulled open and slammed shut each drawer until she came to the bottom one. My mother gasped as she opened the jewelry box that lay hidden among my things. She kneeled down and drew out the necklace with a trembling hand. The scarlet jewel dangled before her eyes. "Asmodeus gave this to you, didn't he?"

"Mom," I croaked. I wanted to say I was sorry, but it was hard to talk. I found myself being dragged along again. This time I didn't fight it. I stumbled as she marched us through the back door to the shed beneath the willow tree. She drew her magic wand and unlocked the shed with a spell.

I blinked in the dusty dimness. My mother let go of my hand and dropped the necklace into the brass bowl on her workbench. She grabbed a few jars and bottles, tossing in some of their contents, and recited a hasty incantation as she waved her wand over the bowl. My brows rose in alarm as multicolored flames billowed. "No, wait! Don't!"

I tried to get past her, but she held me back. Moments later, the flames died down. But the necklace was still intact. It wasn't even scorched—the gold gleamed.

"It's too powerful," my mother muttered, snatching it from the bowl. She glanced around the shed. With a twirl of her wand, a metal lockbox in the corner floated upward, unlocking itself and dumping its contents on the floor as it hovered to her beckoning hand. She threw the necklace inside the box, and the lid latched itself shut. My mother flicked the wand again, and the padlock hanging from the chain on the bookcase clicked open. The chain undid itself, clinking as it slithered like a snake out from the handles, and the glass paneled doors swung open. She pointed the wand, and the box flew to the highest shelf, landing with a thunk. The doors slammed shut, and the chain wove itself through the handles again, the padlock snapping into place once more.

I pressed my hands against the glass of the bookcase doors. From within, I could still feel the soothing calm that emanated from the amulet, but just barely. My mother pulled me away from the bookcase. She grasped me by the chin, forcing me to look at her. She had tears in her eyes. "I told you this would happen. I told you magic would corrupt you."

With a cry, I shoved my way past my mother, dashing out of the shed and back inside the house. I stomped into my bedroom and collapsed onto my bed, my chest heaving as tears rolled down my cheeks.

* * *

Three days later, the murmur that filled the cafeteria quieted a little as I stepped through the doors. I kept my gaze on the floor, avoiding the stares from my classmate as I strode quickly to my lunch table.

Before I could get there, I saw a pair of hooves emerging from frayed jeans. I looked up at Murk. He frowned at me before stepping out of my path.

I blinked. "No quips today, Murk? You're not gonna make a 'speak of the devil' pun?"

"Stay away from me, freak," he grumbled, hurrying away.

I continued to my table. Zack and Jeremy were already seated there. I set my lunch box down across from them, avoiding eye contact.

"You okay, Lesley?" Zack asked. "I heard you got suspended. What happened?"

"I don't want to talk about it." I sighed and glanced around the room. A few classmates were still whispering to one another. "What are they saying about me?"

Jeremy hesitated. "All sorts of rumors are flying around, but they can't really be true."

"What kind of rumors?"

He glanced at Zack, then at me. "That you've been sacrificing small animals in the woods, or that you're in league with the devil himself, or that you aren't just *half* demon. Supposedly, Pauline has a video of whatever it is you did that got you suspended, but she's too scared to show anyone." Jeremy shook his head. "I'm sure whoever started these nasty rumors is just being mean." His gaze flickered toward Nerissa's table. "Really, *really* mean."

I glanced away. "Yeah, none of those rumors are true." *Except for the part about Pauline having video evidence.*

A moment later, Sadie stepped through the cafeteria entrance. Our eyes met, but Sadie tore her gaze away from mine. She headed across the cafeteria and sat down at a table by herself.

* * *

Gray light seeped through the leafless branches. A layer of snow covered the forest floor and dusted the stones of the old, lone chimney. I sat on a log at the edge of the clearing, hugging myself. The air against my face was cold except for where the warm streaks of tears trickled down.

Footsteps crunched across the snow, and I looked up as Zack approached.

"I thought I'd find you here." He sat on the log next to me. "You didn't come to the library after school. What's wrong?"

I sniffed and wiped my eyes. "Everyone thinks I'm a freak."

"I don't think that," Zack said.

"Then why don't you—" I bit my lip. *Then why don't you like me?* I took a breath, trying to keep myself from bursting into tears again. "Zack, I'm half demon. What else am I but a freak? I wish I could just run away, but I can't go back to the human world—not when I look like this."

"What about your lessons with Balthazar? Didn't he teach you anything that could help?"

I shook my head. "I'm the same as you, Zack. I don't have the aptitude for witchcraft. I can't do anything useful with it."

He was quiet for a long time. Zack chewed his lip like he didn't know what to say.

"Don't worry about me, Zack," I said, breaking the silence. "I just want to be alone right now, okay?"

He swallowed. "Okay, Lesley." Slowly, he got up and trudged across the clearing. He glanced back at me, still biting his lip in worry, before heading off down the trail.

Moments later, I noticed Caelum watching me from among the trees. "What a nice young man that was," he said, stepping out. "Would you like me to teach you how to seduce him?"

That was a weird, awkward thing for a dad to say, but then again, Caelum was a tempter demon. "Leave me alone," I growled.

"I couldn't help but overhear," he continued. "If you truly feel out of place here, then come with me. Come to the Scholomance."

"Did you also overhear the part where I said I want to be alone?" I rose and turned to leave.

He caught me by the shoulder, "Lesley, please—"

"Let me go!" I slipped out of his grip, but he appeared in front of me in a whiff of smoke and flame.

His eyes were pleading. "Why won't you come with me?"

"You really wanna know why? You say you want to help me, but you somehow *can't* because of some magical contract. Whatever you say doesn't matter because you're doing a *great* job showing me what being a slave of Asmodeus is like." I crossed my arms, turning away. "Mom fought demons to rescue me, but all *you* can do is talk."

I expected him to poof into existence in front of me again, telling me yet another lame reason I should come with him, but he didn't. Instead, Caelum was silent for a long moment.

"I remember that day," he said finally. "A gaggle of nurse demons had come to take you down to Hell. Before they arrived, your mother confessed to me that she'd been having second thoughts about letting them take you. Then, once the nurse demons gathered around to examine you…" He let out a breath. "I was stunned more by Jane's betrayal than by the spell she cast on me. She knocked out most of others before they could react, then took you away." I turned to face him and was almost startled to see tears in his eyes. "You're my child too."

I gaped, unsure what to say. Part of me warned this could be a trick to gain my sympathy, but the rest of me wasn't listening.

Caelum quickly composed himself. "You have such strength. The path before you is bent and twisted, but I believe you are clever enough to find a way on your own. I truly wish I could help you more directly, but as I've said, I am bound by my contract with Asmodeus."

I blinked. "Wait… you think I can find the shapeshifting spell *myself*?" I shook my head. "Even if I could, I won't be able to cast it. Mom took away my amulet."

He shook his head. "You are not powerless. Magic flows within your very blood. You have enough to cast basic spells such as the one for unlocking, which you can use to get your amulet back."

I shivered, remembering how I had traded a blood sample to Balthazar in exchange for witchcraft lessons. The warlock had said cambion blood was a powerful magical ingredient.

"However," Caelum continued, "I must warn you that drawing directly upon your blood is dangerous. Doing so will burn your blood, which will slowly poison you. You must be very careful not to do so too much or too often."

Outwardly, I remained still, but inside, my emotions clashed. Finally, I shook my head. "No! This is a trick. You're just trying to trick me!" I stomped past him, heading for the trail through the woods.

"Lesley!" Caelum called after me. "However this ends—whether you join us or not—know that I truly do care about you."

I looked back over my shoulder at him, but shook my head again and turned away.

17

The Hellhound

Snow crunched beneath my boots as I trudged along the trail through the woods. The skeletal branches of the trees bent under the weight of the snow clinging to them. The sky was overcast, and the air was perfectly still and quiet. Rugby trotted at my side, his breath fogging the air. Zack followed just behind. My hands were buried in the pockets of my coat, and I wore earmuffs—my horns made it awkward to wear a hat.

I looked down at Rugby. "You're not really here to protect me from Asmodeus, are you?" I shook my head. "As if you could even do such a thing. I saw how scared you were of him. No. Mom is actually sending you to *spy* on me, isn't she?"

The black-and-white dog peered up at me, panting.

"Don't try to be cute with me. I know you're on her side."

Zack stepped up next to me. "Lesley, stop. Your mom just wants you to be safe." He placed a hand on my shoulder. "You're really lucky to have a mother who loves you. Be thankful for that."

Zack himself hadn't been so lucky. I stopped walking. "I—you're right, Zack. I should be thankful she cares enough to…" I sighed. Part of me knew what my mother had done was for the best, and I tried to convince myself everything would be okay in the end. But without my amulet—without magic—I felt a hole in my heart.

I faced Zack, looking into his eyes. "I'm thankful for you, too. For our friendship, I mean." I swallowed nervously. "Zack, I wanted to tell you—"

But he was looking past me at something. "Lesley—" Zack pointed, his hand shaking.

A rasping growl came from the trees nearby. I gasped as a huge black hound crept out of the woods. The creature was like a shadow, pitch black even in the gray afternoon light. Its eyes blazed with fire, and the snow beneath its paws sizzled and melted. It snarled, a glow like a furnace seeping between its jagged teeth.

"Lesley," Zack quavered, "what is that?"

"It's a hellhound," I murmured.

Rugby growled at the intruder. His leash slipped from my hand as he dashed forward, placing himself between me and the shadowy creature, snarling and barking. I remembered what my mom had told me to do. I ran after him, reaching for Rugby's collar, but the hellhound lunged, its jaws snapping. Its hot breath washed over me, carrying the rotten-egg stink of sulfur. With a scream, I reeled back as the hound lunged past Rugby.

I scrambled away from the demonic hound. "Zack!" I cried. "His collar!"

Zack's eyes were wide with alarm. "What?"

"Rugby's collar! Take it off him!"

Zack undid the collar around Rugby's neck, and Rugby launched himself at the hellhound. As he did, fire sprang up around the dog. Rugby's vicious barking grew deeper. Within the flames, his silhouette grew larger. A second later, he was the size of a horse. The flames winked out, and

Rugby's hulking, shadowy form loomed over the other creature. Three pairs of burning eyes blinked down, and searing heat hissed out through three sets of wicked jaws.

The other hellhound peered up at Rugby. It snarled, and flames swirled around it as it grew larger, nearly matching Rugby in size. When the flames went out, a second head peered from atop the beast's broad shoulders. The two-headed hellhound faced the three-headed one and lunged.

Unearthly noises echoed through the forest as the hellhounds fought. Jaws snapped and flames hissed. Claws scratched, gouging bark from trees and tearing at shadowy hide. Drops of black blood fell, sizzling as they hit the snow. Finally, the two-headed hound relented, whimpering and shrinking back to its original size as it fled into the forest.

Rugby peered down at me, tilting his three huge heads. Fire engulfed him, and his silhouette shrank down again. When the flames went out, he had only one head and was covered in his usual coat of black-and-white fur. I took the collar from Zack and, with shaking hands, buckled it around Rugby's neck.

Zack peered at the dog, his eyes wide. "Rugby is a hellhound too?"

"Yeah. I guess it *was* a good thing my mom sent him with us." I backed away as Rugby tried to nuzzle my knees. My mom said she couldn't get rid of Rugby because he was bound to her soul, but had reassured me he was completely loyal and would never hurt me. I'd known this for a while, but I hadn't seen Rugby's true form until now. I doubted I'd ever look at him the same way again.

I pulled my phone from my pocket. A hellhound attack wasn't something I could just not tell her about. "Mom? Come quick, something's happened. No, no... me and Zack are fine. Just get here as fast as you can."

Zack was still staring at Rugby. He peered out at the woods. "Why did that thing come after us?"

"Someone sent it after me. Remember that black-cloaked freak in these woods? I saw them again, and they were trying to summon a hellhound. They must have finally figured out how."

"We still haven't figured out who that was, though."

I narrowed my eyes. "I think we know *exactly* who would do something like this to me."

We headed along the trail to a spot where there was an opening in the trees and waited, looking up at the gray sky. Within a couple of minutes, something came gliding over the treetops. It was my mother riding on her old-fashioned broomstick. She dove between the trees, kicking up snow as she skidded to a stop along the path. She looked at me. "What's wrong, sweetie?"

"A hellhound attacked us!" I pointed back down the path. "It was just over there."

"A hellhound?" She turned to Zack. "You're both okay?"

Zack nodded. "Your familiar spirit, Rugby, he fought it off." He glanced at the dog again, this time with wonder in his eyes. "He was amazing! Thank goodness you sent him with us."

My mother drew her wand from her coat. She carried her broom like a walking stick, leading me and Zack along the trail. Rugby kept close to my mother's side, ears perked forward.

As we approached the spot where the fight had occurred, I blinked in confusion. All signs of the struggle had disappeared—no gouged bark or snapped branches, no melted patches in the snow. Instead, two pairs of boot tracks and one set of paw prints led along the trail, as if Zack, Rugby, and I had simply been strolling along.

"What the…" Zack murmured.

"It was right here," I blurted. "I swear it was!"

My mother faced me. The concern in her expression was gone. "If you think you can scare me into giving back that amulet—"

"No! Mom, I'm telling the truth. You have to believe me!" I turned to Zack. "You saw it too, didn't you?"

He nodded. "Mrs. Robinson—"

"Lesley!" my mother snapped. "If you're *lying* to me again, I swear I'll—" She blinked, her anger fading. "No, this is one of his tricks." She faced the trees. "You won't drive a wedge between us, Asmodeus!" she called out. "You won't—" She sniffed, wiping her eyes. "Sweetie, I'm sorry for yelling at you. I'm so sorry." She hugged me close, her warm tears on my neck.

* * *

Jeremy looked startled. "A *hellhound* attacked you?"

I nodded from across the lunch table. "I'm just glad Rugby was there to fight it off."

He glanced between me and Zack. "And you think this black-robed figure is who summoned it? Who do you think it was?"

I drew my brows together. "Who else could it be? Can you think of anyone else we've seen sneaking into the woods and pranking me with magic spells? It was Nerissa!"

"It probably was her," Zack agreed.

Jeremy swallowed nervously. "Then… then we need to expose Nerissa somehow." He rose from his seat.

"Where are you going?" I asked.

He glanced back at me. "I think I know who can help us."

Zack and I followed Jeremy past the other tables. I slowed, hesitating as the two boys approached Sadie, sitting by herself.

She avoided making eye contact with me. "What is it?" Sadie said to Jeremy.

"Lesley and Zack were attacked by a hellhound!" Jeremy blurted.

Sadie's eyes widened. "Oh my god. Are you guys okay?"

"We're fine," Zack said.

Finally, Sadie glanced at me. I looked away, too nervous to say anything.

"We think Nerissa summoned it," Jeremy explained. "If she's been using black magic, then holy water should burn her, shouldn't it?"

Sadie's gaze grew distant. "Holy water. Yeah, it hurts sorcerers as well as the undead." She paused. "You want me to get some for you, don't you?"

"You know how the principal is. She isn't gonna do anything about this." Jeremy hesitated. "That means it's up to us. We need to show everyone Nerissa is a sorceress."

Sadie paused. "Okay," she said finally. "I'll get in touch with the Slayers Guild and see if they'll lend me some." She didn't look very eager though.

Zack raised an eyebrow. "The Slayers Guild?"

"Monster hunters," Sadie explained. "We tip them off about soulless or otherwise troublesome vampires, and in return, the Guild leaves the rest of us alone." She shook her head. "But those guys still give me the creeps!"

I could tell she wasn't kidding. And if she could do this for me, I hoped it meant our friendship could be repaired.

"Okay," said Jeremy, "let's say we get some holy water. Then what? We still need a plan for how to expose Nerissa."

* * *

A couple days later, on the way to the cafeteria, I passed beneath a banner hung across the hallway. It was decorated with cutouts of snowflakes in shades of blue and white. Letters cut from construction paper announced the upcoming Yule Dance.

I overheard two girls talking. "So who do you want to go to the dance with?" the feathery-winged girl asked her friend.

"I wouldn't mind if that werewolf on the Faeball team asked me," the fox-eared girl replied.

The harpy crooked an eyebrow. "You mean Jeremy? Have you seen him in his human form? He's kinda… wimpy looking."

"Maybe, but his werewolf form is nice. Say, when is the dance coming up, anyway?"

"Duh, it's on the night of the winter solstice."

Their conversation faded into the distance as I wandered past. I shivered. *The winter solstice. Was it really coming up that soon?*

I joined the crowd as my classmates meandered into the cafeteria. I sat with Zack and Jeremy at our usual table, nervously watching the entrance. Finally, Sadie stepped through. For once, she came over to our table instead of going to sit alone. She sat across from me, avoiding eye contact as she set down her thermos.

"Were you able to get the holy water?" Jeremy asked her.

Wordlessly, Sadie opened her purse and took out a glass vial suspended on a chain. She held it like she was holding a dead rat by the tail.

Zack glanced awkwardly between the two of us. Jeremy leaned toward Sadie. "You wanna tell me what this beef between you and Lesley is about?"

I looked at her. "Sadie, I—"

Sadie met my gaze with narrowed eyes. "I promised not to talk about it," she said to Jeremy, "and a vampire always keeps her promises." She threw back her head, taking a long swig from her thermos.

As if I needed a reminder I'd broken my promise to not use magic. Several seconds of silence ticked by. Finally, Zack cleared his throat. "So, Lesley, the Yule Dance is coming up next week."

Every nerve in my body went on high alert. "Is it?" I asked, trying to be nonchalant.

"Yeah. There's someone I want to ask to go with me. I get kind of awkward when it comes to that sort of thing, though. Could you give me some advice on how to ask her out?"

"Oh, I see." I held my wings against my back to keep them from drooping in disappointment. "Is it that one witch-girl, Helen? I guess she seems like your type."

Zack paused. "No, actually, it's someone else."

Someone else. I bit my lip, trying not to frown. "I'm kinda awkward with that sort of thing, too, Zack. I wouldn't know what advice to give."

Jeremy looked between me and Zack. "The dance. Guys, that's it!"

I blinked at him. "What do you mean?"

"That's how we can expose Nerissa. Everyone will be there. If we throw the holy water in Riss's face at the dance, everyone will see." Jeremy grinned. "And we can take a video of it too!"

"What, is she gonna melt like the Wicked Witch of the West?" Zack asked.

"No, it'll just burn her a little," Jeremy explained.

For what felt like the first time in days, I smiled. "I like this plan, Jeremy. I can't wait to see the look on Principal Constance's face when Nerissa—ow!"

Someone had stepped on my tail. I yanked in the wayward appendage, wrapping it around my shins, before turning to find Nerissa behind me. "Oh, sorry," she said, continuing past. She headed to one of the other tables, joining Pauline and Daphne.

Beneath the table, the barbed tip of my tail lashed. I clenched my fists, trying hard not to scream. "Stupid Nerissa," I muttered under my breath, along with other unkind words. Something flashed through my mind—the magic word my subconscious had whispered during Nerissa's ballet performance, the curse to inflict pain. I still remembered what it was. Before I realized it, my lips formed themselves around the syllables, and I silently mouthed the magical curse. Of course, even if it was a magic word and not just gibberish, it still wouldn't do anything—not when I didn't have my amulet. Still, it left a bad taste in my mouth, like I'd dropped the F-bomb.

As the lunch period went on, Zack and Jeremy whispered back and forth, planning what would happen at the dance, while Sadie continued to ignore me. I only vaguely paid attention to them. My anger toward Nerissa still simmered within me.

Then I heard her scream.

My eyes widened. Nerissa had fallen to the floor and was doubled over in pain. Miniature bolts of scarlet lightning arced from her body. The crimson electricity jolted from her to the floor and to the metal legs of the table and the nearby seats. A few seconds later, it ceased. Nerissa stared down at herself. "What the hell?" She started to rise to her feet but screamed once more, sinking to her knees as red lightning jolted from her again.

After a few seconds, the scarlet electricity stopped. Pauline kneeled down, taking Nerissa by the wrists to help her up, but this only got Pauline shocked as well when the red energy surged once more.

Everyone in the cafeteria was watching in stunned silence. "I'll go get help," one of the students said, bounding off down the hallway.

The bursts of energy hit Nerissa several more times before Principal Constance hurried in, followed by the heroic student and the school nurse. The nurse—who was also a witch—spread her hands over the elf-girl.

"She's been cursed," the nurse told Principal Constance. She took out a magic wand, murmuring a spell as she waved it over Nerissa. The nurse's eyes shone with witch-fire, and the lights in the room flickered and dimmed.

After a pop and a shower of red sparks, the fluorescent lights came back on. Nerissa looked down at herself apprehensively, waiting for the next surge, but after several seconds, nothing happened. She sighed and allowed Pauline to help her up from the floor.

Moments later, the bell rang, signaling the end of lunch period. But no one rushed from their seats—everyone was still stunned by what had happened. Finally, after a long silence, people slowly shuffled out of the cafeteria, murmuring to one another as they did. Nerissa spoke quietly with the nurse and the principal.

She turned, pointing an accusing finger at me. "No, it was her!" Nerissa shouted. "It was the demon girl!"

My eyes widened. Some of my classmates turned their gazes toward me.

The principal strode over to my table, high heels clicking across the floor. She crossed her arms. "I have been assured, Miss Robinson, that your source of magic has been taken away and you are unable to cast spells." Mrs. Constance leaned in closer. "But if I learn you caused this incident, I will have you expelled from this school." With that, she marched away.

"So that explains it," Jeremy murmured. He looked at me, taken aback. "I had my suspicions. Maybe I just didn't want to believe it."

I swallowed. "Jeremy, what do you mean?"

"I should have known you'd try to get back at Nerissa. It was no accident when she fell at the talent show, was it? And now this. You've been doing the very same thing back to Nerissa that she did to you. Lesley, I can't—" He shoved back from the table, fists clenched as he strode away through the crowd.

"But I couldn't have." I tried to call after him, but my voice came out in a shaky whisper. "I don't have my..." My eyes widened as I remembered what Caelum had told me. *You are not powerless. Magic flows within your very blood.*

Sadie was watching me with an uneasy expression. "Was it you?" she asked.

My voice quavered. "I-I don't know."

* * *

The last bell of the day rang. I hung my head as I plodded through the crowded hallway. Out of the corners of my vision, I noticed my classmates looking at me funny—some with wariness, others with contempt. I tried to ignore them.

I paused at a junction. A moment later, I turned, heading in a different direction than usual. I peered through the crowd and saw Pauline at her locker. Hesitantly, I approached. "Pauline? I'm looking for Nerissa. I want to... apologize."

Her hooves clopped as she turned to face me. "Riss got sent home early thanks to you, freak." She turned away again, almost hitting me with a swish of her tail.

With a sigh, I slunk back through the crowd the way I had come.

I reached my locker and unslung my satchel, but when I looked up, my brows rose. A note was taped to my locker door. I unfolded the note. As my eyes darted over the handwriting, my brows climbed even higher.

I will make you pay for what you did to me.

As soon as I had read the last word, the paper burst into flame. I yelped, dropping the note. The paper was engulfed before it even hit the floor, the fire winking out as abruptly as it had appeared. I blinked down at the floor—the note was simply gone, not even leaving ashes behind.

18

Transfiguration

My satchel lay by my feet where I'd tossed it carelessly, spilling books onto the floor. A textbook I was supposed to be reading lay to one side of my desk, ignored. Instead, my eyes were focused on the pages of my diary, pages which I almost tore as I turned them. My tail lashed, its barb threatening to rip the hem of my bedspread.

My mom had said journaling would help, but as I read my diary, it only reminded me of all the bad things that had happened. I'd learned I was part demon. I'd been whisked away from the human world without a chance to say goodbye to my best friend. I'd been misunderstood, bullied, called a freak. I'd made enemies and lost most of my new friends. I'd been attacked by a hellhound and by a freaking *dragon* that came to life out of a library book! And yet, somehow, I was expected to study calmly for midterm exams? With a scowl, I slammed the diary shut and shoved it and the textbook off my desk for good measure. I didn't know what to do or where to turn for help.

I blinked. My last encounter with Caelum drifted up from the depths of my memory. Something about what he'd said nagged at me. Caelum had wished he could help me directly.

Was that a hint that he was trying to help *indirectly*? What else had he said?

The path before you is bent and twisted. It seemed an unnecessarily flowery way to say my situation sucked, but I hadn't thought much of it at the time. Maybe, because of the magic of his contract with Asmodeus, he couldn't just tell me, but had to be tricky with his words. *A bent and twisted path... what could he mean by that?*

My eyes widened. *Of course!* A bent and twisted path, like a maze... like the Labyrinth among the bookshelves of the library. And the Labyrinth connected to all libraries across the world—including, I hoped, the one at the Scholomance.

My hands trembled as I pulled my phone from my pocket. "Hello, Phyllis?"

"Lesley!" my friend piped cheerfully through the speaker.

"Hi. Um, can we talk right now?"

"Of course. What's up?"

A knot formed in my stomach. "So, um, my situation right now is... complicated."

"What do you mean?"

"It's hard to explain." I drew in a breath. "I might need to get away from this place. If I'm able to, can I stay with you for a while?"

After a long pause, Phyllis replied. "Are you talking about running away?"

* * *

Winter sunlight slanted through the library windows. I looked at the aisle beneath the sign that said *Metaphysics*. It seemed like as good a place as any to start. With each step, the aisle stretched longer until the far end had vanished into the distance.

I came to a side passage. Within, vines clung to the shelves, and further down, flowers and tufts of grass had burst through the carpet. The sign above the entrance read *Herbalism*. I tried to remember how it felt to be in the Scholomance library, hoping the feeling would guide me. I continued on and came to another opening in the bookshelves. Beyond, the air seemed filled with rays of rainbow light, as if the sun were shining through stained glass. The sign above the entrance said *Spirituality*. I paused and passed by the opening.

I came to another passage but almost missed it because of how narrow it was. Within, the shadows seemed darker than usual. Something about it reminded me of the Scholomance. I looked up at a sign that read *Demonology*. I drew in a breath and stepped into the narrow aisle. As I did, I could have sworn the sign above me changed to *Abandon Hope All Ye Who Enter Here*.

The shelves stood oppressively close at either side, and I had an uneasy feeling that they were slowly closing in. I squared my shoulders, marching onward. The shelves grew more dusty the further I went, the books on them appearing old and tattered. The light grew dimmer. "*Lux*," I said reflexively, holding out my hand. But of course nothing happened—I didn't have my amulet, and I didn't want to try drawing power from my blood just yet. I tried to use my phone as a flashlight, but it didn't work either—there was too much magic in this place. Slowly, I felt my way along through the shadows.

Musty, mildew-covered books lay haphazardly on shelves draped in cobwebs. Beneath my feet, the carpet was tattered and threadbare. Patches were missing, revealing a cobblestone floor beneath. As I crept along, the carpet became more torn and tattered, until only cobblestones remained.

Ahead, the light grew brighter. Around a corner, torches lined the shelves, mounted in rusty iron brackets. Guttering flames danced atop the torches, dripping bits of burning tar and emitting pools of dull, orange light. Around them, shadows danced among the shelves. I continued along the torch-lit aisle, my tail swishing uneasily.

Firelight came from within an opening to one side—real, bright firelight, not like the sickly glow of the torches. Beyond the opening, the books on the shelves were stacked neatly and free of dust. I crept to the far end of the aisle and peeked out. Beyond the rows of shelves, grotesque chandeliers hung from a vaulted ceiling, above tables that surrounded a fire pit. This was it—I'd found the library at the Scholomance.

The room was empty. I listened for a good minute at least, but nobody else seemed to be there. I tiptoed out from the safety of the shelves and saw the red-dyed, gold lettered book in the same spot as before.

I ducked back behind the shelves as footsteps approached outside. The door creaked open, and I heard heavy, inhuman breathing. I grabbed my tail to hold it still. After a long couple of seconds, the door clicked shut again, and the footsteps trudged away outside. Shakily, I reached up and grabbed the book. The lettering of its title, *Spells and Magic of Incubi and Succubi,* gleamed in the firelight. I flipped through the book's yellowed pages, skimming the text, and came to a list of spells. My eyes widened at the one titled *Transfiguration.* I read the description—yes! It was the shapeshifting spell!

I'd thought about just grabbing the book and running, but I *really* didn't want to mess this up. I was worried there might be some kind of magical security measure, like the book would burst into flames as soon as it left the library or something. I took a notebook from my satchel and carefully copied the strange words of the spell. I read it over several times to make sure it was right. Finally convinced it was, I flipped through the book in search of other useful spells.

Behind me, I heard the door swing open again, followed by the sound of clanking footsteps. Someone sniffed the air, and a rasping voice called out, "Oh, it's you! The little thief!"

I bit my lip, stifling a scream. I tried to take the spellbook, but it wouldn't budge—it was being held in place by invisible forces. It seemed I'd been right about there being security measures. I shoved my notebook in my satchel and fled into the Labyrinth. The torch-lit aisle twisted and turned as I ran. After a minute, I leaned back against the shelves to catch my breath. With trembling hands, I checked inside my satchel, peering at the spell I'd written in the notebook.

I jumped as the guard's voice echoed through the maze. "Come out, come out," the goblin rasped.

The floor shook. A rumble filled the aisle, followed by a rattle of pebbles and grit falling to the cobblestones below. The tremor subsided after only a moment, but it had set my pulse pounding. I hurried off down the aisle.

I leaned against the shelves to steady myself as the floor shook again. This time, the shaking continued. Ahead of me, a fiery glow spilled out from a crack in the floor. I watched in horror as the fissure split wider, tearing its way up through the bookshelves. Cobblestones tumbled down into the widening chasm, down to hissing flames and bubbling lava in the depths below. The goblin's laughter echoed through the darkness. "Did you really think this path would be unprotected? We have magic wards to catch little thieves like you!"

My heart raced. I closed my eyes, trying to envision the library back in Misty Hollow. But when I opened them again, I was still standing at the brink of the fiery chasm. It wouldn't work unless I was calm. Unless I could clear my mind, which seemed impossible at the moment, I was stuck here.

The chasm was still widening. Inch my inch, the floor fell away, the brink creeping closer as books and cobblestones tumbled down toward the lava. The goblin's footsteps thumped closer, his breath rasping as he sniffed the air. "This place is only half-real," he cackled. "These paths can easily be bent to trap you. You will find no way out, little thief."

The Labyrinth might not be as real as the physical world, but it was still real enough, I knew all too well. In a panic, I glanced this way and that along the aisle and across to the gaping fissure. My tail lashed, and my wings unfurled involuntarily—

My wings. I looked up at the bookshelves to one side and clambered up as fast as I could. I climbed using my wings as well as my arms and legs, hooking the thumb-claws onto one shelf, then the next. I didn't have time to appreciate it in the moment, but my claws made climbing a lot easier. Once I gained what I hoped was enough height, I swung my satchel back and forth and hurled it over the chasm. It landed with a thunk on the far side.

A cloud of sulfurous fumes billowed past me, stinging my eyes and making me cough. I blinked the tears away and peered across the chasm again. I swallowed, gripping the shelf tightly as I spread my wings. I deeply regretted that this would only be my third attempt at flying, after chickening out on the first one and getting blown down by the wind on the second. I squinted, trying to judge the distance to the other side of the chasm.

I screamed as the shelf I was clinging to cracked. One end tilted down toward the fissure, knocking over books and sending them sliding off the end, plummeting into the fire below. My heart hammered, my knuckles turning white. The wood creaked as books fell on either side of me. I clenched my teeth and kicked away from the shelf, twisting my body toward the chasm as I stretched my wings.

My stomach tied itself in knots. I kept my gaze on the bookshelves on the opposite side, not daring to look down. Sweat beaded on my face as I passed through a plume of scorching heat and reeking smoke. The floor on the far side of the chasm rushed toward me. I screamed, flinging my arms forward.

Miraculously, I didn't slam face first into the floor. Instead, I somehow caught hold of a bookshelf several feet above it. I hung there for a moment, eyes wide in astonishment, and lowered myself down. I gasped for breath, my pulse still pounding as I stood on shaky legs. *Did I actually fly?*

The goblin's footsteps thumped closer, and he appeared through the smoke rising from the chasm. He peered in disbelief across the fissure at me and howled with rage. I grabbed my satchel, running as fast as I could back the way I had come through the Labyrinth.

* * *

Daylight was fading by the time I got back from the library. I stood beneath the old chimney in the clearing, watching my breath rise as puffs of vapor in the air. My insides quivered as I peered at the notebook in my hands. Finally, I turned to the page where I had written the transfiguration spell.

I slowly read the sequence of strange words. As soon as I had finished, a pricking sensation passed over me. My eyes widened, and I screamed as red fire burst from the ground where I stood. The searing, scarlet flames slithered across my skin.

I sank to my knees, my scream echoing through the woods. After a second that felt like an eternity, the fire went out. I looked around in astonishment—the snow at my feet had not melted, and neither my skin nor clothes nor the notebook in my hands were burned or even singed. I heaved a breath of cold air into my lungs.

Slowly, I reached up to touch my forehead. "No!" I drew my shaking hands back from the horns jutting from my brow. I swung my tail forward—it was still there, too—and glanced over my shoulders at my wings. The spell hadn't worked. Tears gathered in my eyes. "No." I wept.

Footsteps came softly across the snow. "A valiant effort," said Caelum, "but transfiguration is a tricky spell. You will first need to master other aspects of sorcery—"

I looked up at him, blinking through the wetness in my eyes. "You knew!" I hissed. "You knew it wouldn't work!"

"Lesley—"

I rose, pointing an accusing finger. "You misled me! You got my hopes up for nothing!"

Caelum reached out. "Lesley, please—"

"Get away from me!" I shrieked. I spun, dashing away across the clearing, back down the snowy path through the forest, wiping tears from my eyes as I ran.

* * *

I stared blankly out my bedroom window, ignoring the textbook that lay open on my desk. The sun was sinking behind the neighbor's roof, its glow shining through the trees and glistening across patches of half-melted snow. Soon, the day would be over. Tomorrow was the winter solstice.

A knock came softly at my bedroom door. "Lesley?" my mother called. "Someone is here to see you."

With a sigh, I rose and went over to the door. When I opened it, Zack stood in the hallway timidly beside my mother.

Zack gave me a shy smile and stepped into my room. I offered him my desk chair and sat down on my bed. My mother peered through the door, smiling, and closed the door most of the way.

"What's this about?" I asked him.

Zack cleared his throat. "I-I'm here to ask you to the dance."

I leaned forward, lowering my voice. "You got Sadie and Jeremy back on board with the plan to expose Nerissa?"

"Yes, but also..." He fidgeted with his glasses. "I want to go to the dance with you."

I crooked an eyebrow. "What happened to that other girl you were interested in?"

He was silent for a moment. "Lesley, I—"

"Zack, are you just trying to make me feel better?"

"No," Zack stammered. "I mean, yes, but also—"

"That's sweet of you, but really, I don't want to go to that stupid dance, anyway."

Zack looked into my eyes. "It was you."

I blinked. "What?"

"The 'other girl' I wanted advice on how to ask out. It was *you*. I was just trying to be covert about it."

My mouth opened, but the words couldn't find their way out at first. "Zack"—I drew in a breath—"does this mean that... that you *like* me?"

He glanced down. "I understand if you don't feel the same way—"

"No! Zack, I *do* feel the same way about you."

He looked up at me. "Really?"

"Yes!" I laughed for what seemed like the first time in days.

A smile spread across his face. He was smiling... because of *me*. "So what do you say?" he asked. "Will you come to the Yule Dance with me?"

I swallowed the lump in my throat. "Yes! Of course I will."

19

Winter Solstice

I stepped out of my mom's car onto the sidewalk in front of the high school. Street lamps cast pools of light along the lane, illuminating the patches of crusty snow that covered the school's front lawn. A fading magenta glow spanned the sky to the west, half obscured by dark clouds rolling in. My breath turned to ghostly vapors in the air. Beneath my coat, I was wearing a dress and high heels, both red to match my tail and wings.

My mother waved to me from inside the car. I smiled, pretending I didn't see the anxious look hiding behind her warm expression. "Have fun, sweetie," she said before driving off.

I turned to face the school building, surprised at how nervous I felt. I'd known Zack ever since coming to Misty Hollow—why should I be nervous around him? I squared my shoulders and marched up the front steps. I used my pocket mirror to do a last-minute makeup check and continued to the gymnasium. Muffled music seeped through the doors, its loudness briefly unleashed as a pair of students ahead of me stepped through. I hesitated. Would Sadie and Jeremy be there? Were they still mad at me? Finally, I pushed my way through the doors.

Music blared from loudspeakers at the far end of the gym. A set of refreshment tables lined one of the walls. Some of my classmates milled about by the refreshments, while others danced to the music. I looked around. Zack wasn't there yet. Neither were Sadie or Jeremy. I tried to stifle the swishing of my tail. Where were they? I peered around the gym again. Nerissa, clad in a sparkling gown, was flirting with one of the centaur boys—or rather, he was flirting with her. I couldn't tell how interested she actually was in him.

I wandered over to the refreshments table. Maybe my friends were just running late. I sent Zack a text and stood awkwardly by the punch bowl. I peered over the rim of my plastic cup as I sipped, searching the room desperately.

Nearly twenty minutes passed. I meandered from one corner of the gym to another, fighting to keep the moisture gathering in my eyes from spilling over. But despite my efforts, a tear trickled down my face. I spun, hurrying back out into the hall.

The sound of my soft, sobbing gasps filled the girls' bathroom. I drew in a ragged breath and looked up into the mirror to see that my makeup was running. I wiped at my face, trying to smudge away the tracks left by the tears, but I stopped, suddenly finding the effort silly. I frowned at the reflection of the horns poking out from my forehead, at the wing-claws jutting up behind my shoulders.

Behind me, the door creaked open. Reflected in the mirror, Pauline and Daphne stepped into the bathroom. I hid my face in my hands as I dashed past them, back out into the hall in search of solitude. I rounded a corner, and I leaned back against the lockers, sinking down to the floor as I burst into tears again.

Some time later, footsteps approached. I sniffed, wiping my nose, and looked up.

With a gasp, I scrambling to my feet.

A figure clad in a black robe had stepped around the corner. Within the hood, their face was wrapped in a black scarf, completely hidden, but around their neck was a gold necklace, a glowing crimson jewel dangling from it. My thoughts raced back to the note I had found on my locker. *I will make you pay.* I screamed as I turned to run.

The dark figure raised a black-gloved hand. A cloying force slithered around my arms and legs, and I couldn't move. I tried to scream again, but the invisible force squeezed around my chest, and all that came out was a wheezing hiss. The figure gestured again, and a nearby door burst open. The forces shoved me inside, and I was slammed back against something hard. Stars danced across my vision.

I blinked, unable to see in the darkness at first, but my eyes began to adjust. Light seeped in through the crack under the door, and I was able to make out the shapes of broom and mop handles—I was in a utility closet. The cloaked figure loomed over me like a shadow. I kicked and scratched uselessly against the wall behind me. The telekinetic grip pressed me against the wall, constricting my chest and crushing the air out of my lungs.

The red glow of the amulet pulsed at the cloaked figure's throat. The calm of its magic brushed against me. In desperation, I reached out and grabbed the dangling gemstone. As my fingers closed around the jewel, its power rushed up my arm, flooding into my body. I moved my lips, silently speaking a magic word. *Praesidium!*

In a crackling flash of red light, the amulet slipped from my grip, and the robed figure was thrown back. They burst through the door, reeling as they stumbled into the hallway. The cloaked figure turned, dashing away.

The telekinesis squeezing my chest had vanished. I drew in a ragged breath, sinking back against the wall. After a few moments, I stood up and peeked through the doorway. But the dark figure had gotten away. I hobbled back into the hallway. Moments later, footsteps came running toward me. I spun in alarm, but it was only Zack. He looked as frightened as I felt.

"Did something happen?" he asked. "I heard a noise."

I glanced past him, drawing my brows together. My words hissed through my teeth. "Yeah, something happened. Nerissa just *attacked* me!"

"Oh my god," Zack murmured. "I don't know where Sadie and Jeremy are. Sadie was supposed to bring the holy water. What should we do?"

"I can't deal with this anymore, Zack." I was surprised at how calm my voice sounded. "It's time I admit Misty Hollow isn't where I belong."

His brows rose in alarm. "Wait, Lesley!"

"Goodbye, Zack." Without looking back at him, I turned and strode resolutely down the hall. I burst through the school's front entrance, stepped out into the frigid night air, and spread my wings.

* * *

Snowflakes drifted from the dark sky, swirling past me as I careened through the air. Flapping my wings unsteadily, I skimmed above roofs and treetops. Snow was falling, but despite the bitter cold, I flew on. I wore a grim expression, my makeup smudged and streaked with tears.

Below, the streetlights gleamed across a quickly accumulating blanket of snow. In the back of my mind, part of me was reeling in astonishment. I was flying! I wanted to scream—maybe in excitement, maybe from sheer terror, maybe both—but the rage seething in my heart held it back.

I approached my house and crooked my wings, tipping into a dive. The ground rushed toward me. I aimed for the backyard and threw my feet forward, kicking up swirls of snow as my high heels hit the ground. But still unused to flying as I was, I stumbled and fell, tumbling and rolling to a stop across the yard.

I climbed to my feet and brushed off some of the snow clinging to my dress, frowning at the torn hem. I turned toward the shed beneath the willow tree, stumbling again as I tried to walk across the snow. I kicked off my high heels, hissing at the chill as I hopped across the snow barefoot.

I hugged myself, shivering as I stood before the shed. Caelum's words echoed in my mind. *Magic flows within your very blood.* I listened to my heartbeat and drew in a breath of the frigid air. A sense of calm came over me—not washing across me like with the amulet but welling up from within. I focused on the door's latch and murmured the words of the unlocking spell.

The latch clicked, and the door creaked open. I stepped inside, peering at the bookcase at the far end of the room. The chains and padlock were still wound through the handles of the shelf's doors. I focused on my heartbeat and repeated the incantation.

This time, my stomach felt queasy. *It will slowly poison you,* Caelum had warned me. *You must be very careful.*

The padlock sprang open, and the chains unwound themselves from the door handles, sliding to the floor in a heap. I stepped up to the bookcase and pulled out the metal lockbox. Inside it, I could feel the power of my amulet, could feel its cold clarity brush across my skin. I cradled the box in my arms as I carried it over to the workbench. I set it down and focused on the keyhole. A third time, I spoke the unlocking spell.

My vision swam as nausea washed over me. I clutched at the edge of the workbench, sinking down to my knees as my stomach lurched. I tasted bile in my throat. After several seconds, the nausea faded. I sucked in a ragged breath and dizzily stood up again. As I looked down at the workbench, my eyes went wide. The lockbox was open. Inside it, the gold chain of the necklace lay coiled around the glowing red jewel. I snatched up the amulet, clasping the chain around my neck, and its power flooded into me.

The amulet whispered something into my mind. I smiled and looked down at myself. "*Contexe igni.*" Warmth spread into my body as threads of fire wove themselves through my veins. The heat washed away the chill that had gripped me, and my numb toes began to tingle. The snow that clung to me melted, wisps of steam rising from my skin and soaked dress. I laughed in delight.

Outside, footsteps came running across the snow, and the shed's door burst open. "Lesley?"

I turned and saw my mother framed by the doorway.

She gasped as she saw the crimson jewel hanging in front of my chest. "Lesley, wait!"

I scowled at her. "*Impulsio!*"

My mother stumbled to the side, and I dashed past her out the door. I leaped into the air, flapping my wings as I climbed above the neighborhood.

"Lesley!" My mother's voice faded into the distance as I flew toward the forest. I circled, gazing down at the dark patch of woods beyond the houses, only a couple of streets away. My wings raked the air, scattering snowflakes falling more heavily than before. Branches rattled as I plunged into the trees. I flared my wings and skidded to a stop along a snowy path through the forest.

I reached out a hand. "*Lux.*" An orb of red light appeared, floating above my palm. I held it out like a lantern as I strode along the trail. I smirked down at the snow, watching it sizzle and melt beneath my bare feet.

Inside my purse, my phone buzzed. It was my mother. I had other missed calls from her and Sadie as well. I scowled, about to chuck the phone into the woods, but I swiped the screen and typed a message to Phyllis. *Thanks for being such a good friend. I promise to see you again in person some day.* Then I tossed the phone over my shoulder and didn't look back.

Before long, I came to the clearing. Snow was piling up on one side of the old chimney. Someone gave a startled yelp. I turned, and the light from my conjured orb glinted off a pair of glasses.

"Lesley," Zack gasped.

"How did you find me?" I growled.

"This is where you always come when you're upset." He swallowed nervously. "What are you doing?"

"I'm going somewhere else, somewhere I actually fit in." I turned, peering out into the darkness among the trees, and drew in a deep breath. "Caelum!"

A man stepped into the pool of light from my conjured orb. "Have you had a change of heart?"

"Who is that?" Zack asked.

"This is my father." I stepped over to Caelum and drew my brows together. "No more disguises. Let me see your true form."

"Very well." He closed his eyes and moved his lips silently in an incantation. Fire burst up, washing across him. Within the flames, his silhouette shifted. His legs elongated and bent, and the spindly struts of wings sprouted behind his back.

The fire went out. Caelum was now dressed only in a tattered loin cloth. His skin was red with an oily, slimy sheen. He stood upon a pair of cloven hooves, and a sinuous, spade-tipped tail swayed behind him. The hooked thumb-claws of his huge, bat-like wings hovered above his shoulders, and his fingernails had become claws as well. His eyes glowed like embers, and upon his brow, poking through oily tangles of jet black hair, was a pair of horns—horns like my own.

"This is what I truly am, my daughter," he said, his voice ringing with unearthly resonance. Caelum glanced at Zack. "I seem to have startled your friend."

Zack had ducked behind the chimney. He peeked out timidly. "Lesley—"

"Don't try to talk me out of this. I've made my decision." I turned back to Caelum. "How do we make this official?"

"We will go to Hell and meet Asmodeus," the incubus explained. "You will sign a contract, pledging your soul to him. Then you will return to Earth and travel to the Scholomance, where your training will begin." He gestured to a spot on the ground. "Would you care to do the honors? I believe you know the spell."

I nodded. Whatever part of me that had been anxious before now felt numb. If becoming a servant of Asmodeus was what it took to find peace, then so be it. I looked to the spot on the ground and reached out my hands. "*Impulsio.*" With one hand, I twisted my fingers, weaving them through the air. Gouges were ripped out of the earth, as if being drawn by huge, invisible claws. One by one, the scratches traced out the angular shapes and runes of a summoning circle. "*Ignis*," I incanted. Seven scarlet flames leaped to life, surrounding the circle etched upon the ground.

Caelum smiled, his sharp teeth glinting. "Nicely done."

I smiled back. Focusing on the summoning circle, I spoke the spell to open the portal. A pillar of fire surged up from the circle, rising above the treetops and casting long, stark shadows through the woods. Hot, sulfurous wind howled, making the leafless branches sway and clatter. I allowed the orb of light in my hand to go out as I stepped over to Caelum. He took me by the hand and led me to the column of fire.

Something darted past overhead. "Lesley!" my mother's voice called down from the sky.

I turned, watching through narrowed eyes as she swooped into the clearing. She tossed her broomstick aside and brandished her wand. My mom scowled at the demon who stood next to me.

A moment later, her expression changed, her eyes growing wide. "Caelum?"

"It's been a long time, hasn't it, Jane?" He let go of my hand and stepped over to her, reaching out to brush her face. "Oh, how I have missed you."

My mother reeled back. She aimed her wand at him. "Let my daughter go!"

Caelum shook his head sadly. "I can't do that. You know I can't, Jane. I'm bound by my contract with Asmodeus, just as you are."

"No! I defied him, didn't I?"

"You may have tried to. And yet, Lesley has come here on this night, just as our master said she would."

"No, I won't let you take her!" My mother thrust the wand forward, and a burst of green fire surged out. Caelum spread his hands, projecting a translucent barrier in front of him until the flames dissipated. He looked at my mother with an expression full of hurt. Slowly, he turned away from her and trudged back to where I stood.

"Lesley!" my mother called, shouting over the wind. "Come back with me! Come home, please!"

"Why? Why do you care so much?" Tears welled in my eyes. "I'm the reason your life was ruined!"

She shook her head. "That doesn't matter. Lesley, please..."

A crash came through the underbrush. Rugby bounded out of the woods and strode up to my mother's side, and Sadie dashed out into the clearing. "Lesley!"

Jeremy, in his shaggy werewolf form, raced after her. He was carrying something, a dark bundle in one of his clawed hands. His brows climbed as he peered up at the pillar of fire surging from the portal.

"Lesley, wait!" Sadie shouted. "Don't! It's a trick. He's tricked you!"

Moments later, my gaze turned past her. My eyes widened as Nerissa stepped out of the trees into the shifting, fiery glow that filled the clearing.

20

Holy Water

I ran to the edge of the snowy clearing to where Nerissa stood. "What the hell is *she* doing here?" I screamed.

Nerissa's eyes went wide in fright. She threw her hands up in front of her. "Lesley, wait! You don't understand!"

My mother and Sadie caught me before I could reach Nerissa. They pulled me back from her as I struggled against their grip. "Let me go!"

"Listen to me, Lesley—" Sadie began.

"Why should I listen to you? You turned your back on me!"

She looked me in the eye. "It wasn't her!"

I blinked, and my struggling lessened. "What?"

"Nerissa isn't a sorceress like we thought."

"But... but she—"

"All that stuff I did was dryad magic," Nerissa explained. "After you hexed me, I stopped using it on you. I swear!"

I stopped struggling. Sadie and my mother released me, and I slowly stepped up to Nerissa. "Prove it! Prove you're not a sorceress."

Sadie came up to her and held out the vial of holy water. It was still about two-thirds full. Nerissa held out her hand, allowing Sadie to drip some of the water onto it.

Nothing happened. "There, you see?" Nerissa said.

My insides were quivering. "But... I found that creepy altar in the ditch. I saw you sneak right past there."

"I didn't build that altar—I didn't even know it was there. That ditch is just the shortcut I take to get into the woods. I like to go there whenever I'm upset. It's so peaceful."

"But in the woods, I saw you in a black robe, reading incantations from a spellbook over a summoning circle. I saw you trying to summon a hellhound. Then, at the dance, you put on that robe again and attacked me!"

Jeremey strode up. He shook his lupine head and held out the bundle in his hand. It was a black, hooded cloak. "Not... her," he growled. He pointed a clawed finger. "Him!"

"Jeremy found this in the hallway at school, stuffed in a trash can," Sadie explained. She glanced toward the chimney. "It has *Zack's* scent on it."

My eyes widened. "No," I quavered. "It can't be..."

"Think about it. Who was with you when you first encountered the dark figure in the woods? *Zack* was. Who was with you when the hellhound attacked? *He* summoned it, knowing Rugby would protect you. And I'll bet anything he cast that curse on Nerissa just to make you feel guilty." She pressed the vial of holy water into my hands. "Go see for yourself."

With trembling fingers, I clutched the vial and strode over to the chimney. Zack peeked out from behind it. "They're lying! Nerissa must... must have them under a spell! She's making them say all that!"

But from the way he wouldn't look me in the eye, I knew he wasn't telling the truth. I felt like I had been punched in the stomach. "Zack," I croaked. "Why?"

"I'm telling you, I didn't—"

My arm snapped forward as I threw the holy water right in his face. Zack screamed. He hid his face in his hands as flames hissed up. The fire quickly went out, and Zack sank to his knees, weeping in pain.

My words hissed through my teeth. "You were never satisfied with not being able to do witchcraft. Asmodeus offered you another way to do magic, didn't he?"

Zack looked up at me. His face was red and blistered. "He did," Zack said through chapped lips.

"He gave you an amulet."

Zack nodded. He reached into the collar of his coat and pulled out a gold chain. A luminous red jewel dangled from it—the same one I'd seen around the dark figure's neck.

"You were the cloaked figure in the woods and in the hallway at school?"

He looked away, nodding again.

"Why, Zack? Why did you trick me?"

"Asmodeus said the only way I could get into the Scholomance was if you came there too."

I backed away a step. "Were... were you just *pretending* to be my friend this whole time?"

He shook his head. "Asmodeus didn't come to me until partway into the semester. I didn't want to trick you, but it was the only way..."

"I thought you *liked* me! Was that a lie too?"

Zack gave me a pleading look. "I *do* like you. I really do. It tore me up inside to have to do those things to you, but... I *had* to. You understand why I had to. I know you do. Wouldn't *you* do anything to get your amulet back?" He rose to his feet. "Please, come with me to the Scholomance. You'll make an amazing sorceress. I really mean that."

A hand settled on my shoulder. "Now you know the truth," Caelum murmured. "Our methods may seem harsh, but in time, you will come to understand."

"Don't touch her!" my mother shouted. She brandished her wand. "She's coming home with me!"

Caelum narrowed his eyes at her. "That is Lesley's decision to make, not yours." He strode to the base of the pillar of fire and looked at me. "What do you say, my daughter? Will you go with her or come with me?"

"No, Lesley!" Sadie called.

"I won't let you take her!" my mother cried. She aimed her wand at Caelum.

Jeremy snarled, and Sadie ran toward me. "Lesley, you can't! Don't do it!"

"Shut up!" I screamed. "Everyone shut up!" The amulet whispered something into my mind. I stomped my foot and yelled the incantation as loudly as I could. "*Circumda praesidio!*"

A wave of red energy radiated across the ground, racing out in all directions. It hit Sadie, knocking her back. The energy formed a circle on the ground and surged upward, trailing a translucent sheet in its wake. Within a few seconds, the barrier closed across the sky, forming a dome that surrounded me, Zack, and Caelum. At the far side of the dome, the fires of the portal to Hell fountained upward.

Outside the barrier, my mother stood looking aghast, and Sadie lay crumpled on the ground, unmoving. Jeremy crouched over Sadie's limp form. He carefully picked her up, cradling her in his arms. He shot me an enraged look through the glassy surface of the barrier and slunk away.

My mother was shouting, but through the barrier, her words were muffled. A moment later, she narrowed her eyes and aimed her wand. Green fire erupted. Red lightning crackled across the dome beneath the wave of flame, but the shield held firm. The fire dissipated, and my mother sank to her knees in exhaustion.

"They don't understand us." Zack's lips were cracked and bleeding. "They won't let us just be ourselves."

Caelum stepped into the portal, becoming a dark silhouette within the pillar of fire. He beckoned, reaching out a clawed hand from the flames. "Come, brave Zack, and come, my beloved Lesley. Let us go greet our master Asmodeus."

Outside the dome, my mother was preparing another volley from her wand. But before she could, Sadie dashed in front of her. She held out her arms as if trying to shield me. My mother shouted for her to get out of the way, but Sadie shouted something back. My mother blinked, looking admonished. She lowered her wand.

"Come on," Zack said to me. "We don't need people like them." He took my hand, pulling me toward the fire.

I hesitated. Sadie kneeled outside the barrier. I couldn't hear what she was saying, but she pleaded, wringing her hands as she peered into my eyes. Next to her, my mother pressed her hands to the dome. She moved her lips, repeating something over and over—not a spell, just words. A moment later, I realized what she was saying. *I love you.*

She's lying, a voice whispered to me out of the amulet around my neck. *Your mother hates you. She regrets ever having you.*

A thought bubbled to the surface of my mind. *She came to rescue me, just like she did when I was a baby. She could have had power as a sorceress, but she chose me instead.* Something warm and wet formed in my eyes.

Zack tugged my hand. "Let's go."

I frowned at him, wrested my hand out of his grip, and reached to undo my amulet's clasp. The necklace hissed threats into my mind. At last, I recognized that voice. "Asmodeus," I hissed.

Without me, the demon prince whispered through the necklace, *you will never be human again.*

I hesitated, my hand trembling. Then I tore open the clasp, and Asmodeus's voice vanished from my mind. I faced my father as he waited amid the surging fire.

"Your place is with us," Caelum called. "The people here will never truly understand you. You will always be seen as an outsider."

"Maybe not everyone will understand. But at least my mom loves me. And my friends, they may have gotten scared, but in the end, they came for me. You, though... you just want to use me!"

"Lesley," the demon pleaded, "I care about you! I truly do. I can teach you how to hide your horns and tail and wings so you may be human again... so you may be happy again. But I cannot do so unless you pledge your soul to Asmodeus!"

"No!" I scowled at the demon within the column of flames. "Go to hell." I held up the amulet in my hand. "*Ignis!*"

Scarlet fire erupted from the amulet. I drew out more and more of its power, coaxing the flames to burn hotter and hotter. The pain was almost unbearable, but I clenched my teeth, holding on to the gold chain. The metal glowed, and jolts of crimson energy flashed from the red jewel. I let out a defiant scream. With a thunderous bang, the jewel shattered.

I stumbled, almost falling to my knees. Broken shards fell through the air, turning black as the power they held dissipated. With no more magic to fuel it, the portal began to collapse.

"No!" Caelum roared as he was sucked down into the earth. The plume of fire sputtered and went out, leaving behind a whiff of sulfurous smoke. Above me, the dome I had conjured was ripping open, dissolving into sparks. Cold winter air rushed in. The shimmering membrane crackled as it shredded apart and finally evaporated into nothing.

The hot, sulfur-laden wind ceased, and flakes of snow fell around me. I glanced at my hand—it was red and raw, but not nearly as badly burned as I had feared. Nothing a witch's salve wouldn't heal. I peered down at the shattered black shards at my feet, lying amid drops of molten gold.

Zack backed away from me, gaping disbelief. He grasped the amulet at his throat.

"You don't need that," I said to him. "You don't need magic to be who you really are."

He backed away further. "No, it's mine! You can't take it away from me!" He turned and ran.

"Zack, wait!" But he didn't look back. My breath caught in my throat as I watched him disappear into the woods. "Zack..." I blinked back tears.

"Lesley!" My mother rushed to me, throwing her arms around me.

I hugged her back, enfolding her in my wings. I rested my head on her shoulder and let the tears flow. "Mom," I croaked. "I'm so sorry..."

"It's okay," my mother said. I let her draw me close, and she kissed me on my forehead, right between my horns. "It's okay, sweetie. Let's go home."

* * *

I glanced through the front windows at the blanket of fresh snow on the lawn, which gleamed beneath the morning sun. My tail swished nervously as I peeked into the foyer from the living room. My mother waited by the front door. There was a knock. My mom checked her watch, deliberately waiting several seconds before she answered. Asmodeus glowered as he stepped inside.

"What was it we agreed upon?" my mom asked. "That you would release me from my contract, and—what was the other part?—something about slinking back to Hell in shame and never troubling us again?"

Asmodeus looked at her with a flat expression. He took the scroll she'd signed from inside his jacket and snapped his fingers with his other hand. The parchment burst into flame, ashes fluttering to the floor.

The demon prince glared at my mother. "Do not think this is over, Jane. I only said *I* would not trouble you again. I said nothing about the other princes of Hell." I shivered as he turned his fierce gaze on me. "Mark my words. One day you will succumb to the darkness that lurks within you. It is only a matter of time."

"Is that so?" My mother crossed her arms. "You don't seem to be aware of just how powerful my daughter really is."

I blinked, gasping at the implication of her words.

"She is still young," Asmodeus said. "She is still weak and foolish. She cannot stand against Hell on her own."

"Perhaps not on her own," my mom said, "but with my help and the help of this community, I believe she can overcome anything you and the others can throw at us."

"No, Jane. You will see! Sooner or later, Lesley's soul will be mine!"

"Really? Would you like to make a wager on that?"

Asmodeus opened his mouth and shut it again. He gave my mother a furious glare and stomped out the door, slamming it behind him.

I turned to my mother. A shiver ran through me, and I wasn't able to tell if it was from fear or excitement. "Mom, does that mean…"

"Yes, sweetie." She scooped me up in a hug. "You destroyed that amulet. You willingly gave up your source of power. I'm no longer afraid magic will consume you. I'll try my best to teach you what I know."

I beamed. "Thank you!" I embraced my mother again, enfolding her in my wings.

* * *

This is the part where I'm supposed to say, "And they lived happily ever after." Well, that's not quite what happened. This isn't just some fairy tale.

Through the cafeteria windows, the sun shone upon the snow. Winter break had come and gone, and the students of Misty Hollow High School had returned to begin the next semester. I stepped past the tables, trying to ignore my classmates' wary glances and the way their conversations quieted down as I passed. Nerissa was sitting with her centaur and fairy friends, as well as the satyr Murk.

I hesitated, but stepped up to them. "Hey…"

Pauline glared at me, and Daphne gave me a mean look. Murk crossed his arms, scowling. The three of them rose, heading for a different table. Nerissa watched me for a moment longer, a mixed expression crossing her face. Finally, she looked away and followed her friends.

My wings drooped. *It's gonna take time,* I reminded myself.

I approached another table and swallowed the lump in my throat. "Hey guys, can I sit with you?"

Sadie and Jeremy looked up at me. Zack wasn't with them—after the night of the winter solstice, no one had seen him in town again. My tail swished nervously as the awkward silence ticked by. Jeremy regarded me with a furrowed brow while Sadie avoided my gaze.

"You're not going to flip out on us or anything, are you?" Jeremy asked.

"Oh, no way. I promise, all that craziness is over now."

Jeremy considered this. He gestured to one of the seats.

I sat, setting my lunch box down. "Sadie, I still haven't gotten a chance to thank you. What you did that night... that's what changed my mind."

She kept her gaze on the tabletop.

"I'm *so* sorry, Sadie," I continued. "When I first came here, you went out of your way to be my friend. I should have told you everything that was going on. I was a total jerk and I totally deserve it if you still hate me for that. But I hope that, maybe someday, we can be friends again."

She looked at me. "Maybe someday," Sadie murmured.

I hesitated a moment. "Guys," I said, suppressing the quaver in my voice, "there's something I want to show you." Not letting the nervousness slow me down, I stood up again and pulled something out of the collar of my shirt. It was a leather band around my neck, with a loop of it tied around an irregularly shaped crystal that glowed faintly from within.

Both Jeremy's and Sadie's eyes widened.

"Another amulet!" yelped Jeremy.

"It's okay," I reassured them. "My mom and I made it together. I didn't have to sell my soul for it or anything."

Jeremy didn't look reassured. "You're not still mad at Nerissa, are you? You're not gonna—"

"No, silly." I allowed the necklace's crystal to hang in front of my chest. "Watch this." Silently, I mouthed the words of a spell.

Crimson flames washed over me, flickering out as quickly as they had appeared. Some of the students at the nearby tables turned, murmuring in surprise. Jeremy blinked. Sadie clapped her hands over her mouth in astonishment.

I glanced behind my back. My wings and tail were gone. I touched my forehead and felt smooth skin all the way across it. I smiled at the werewolf and the vampire as they gaped at me. "My mom helped me figure out the shapeshifting spell."

"Oh my god, Lesley," Sadie murmured.

I twirled, allowing my friends to see my restored human form. "However…" I whispered a spell again. Once more, a flicker of scarlet fire passed over me. When it faded, my horns, tail, and wings had reappeared. "That's not who I really am."

Sadie rose from her seat, her eyes wide. "But… ever since you came to Misty Hollow, all you wanted was to be human again."

I shrugged. "I guess I've decided being a freak isn't so bad after all." I smiled at her. "I shouldn't be ashamed of what I really am, right? And, after all, I'm only half human."

About the Author

Nathaniel has been writing ever since he was little. After finishing his bachelor's degree, he decided to take his childhood hobby more seriously, and tried to write an action-adventure novel involving vampires and half-demons. Later, he read Harry Potter and decided Young Adult was more his style. But he didn't give up on vampires or half-demons.